PAYBACK JACK

A VIGILANTE JUSTICE THRILLER

J.E. TRENT

FOREWORD

PRAISE FOR J.E. TRENT

J.E. Trent spins a riveting, unputdownable tale, that brings a moral dilemma for our hero - how far is he prepared to go, to enact payback on behalf of those who can't defend themselves?

Perfect for fans of David Berens, Luke Richardson and Clive Cussler. –Rosemary Kenny

Also by J.E. Trent

Hawaii Action Adventure Series
Book 1 Death in Paradise
Book 2 Death Orchid
Book 3 The Kona Strangler
Book 4 Death Tide

Visit my website JeTrentBooks.com for the latest release.

CHAPTER ONE

After I fueled the boat, I put it back inside its slip at the harbor and went into the salon with coffee in one hand and the Sunday paper in the other.

Usually, I liked to sit in the fighting chair in the cockpit and read the paper, but it was windy and sprinkling. The forecast was to drop an inch of rain. From the looks of the dark sky, it wouldn't be long before it poured. Warm rain was ok, I loved the smell of it, just not when outside trying to read the paper.

I sat on the couch and glanced at the headline. It read, *Another homeless man found stabbed to death in the village.* I shook my head in disbelief. The crime was so heinous and the act so foreign to my little slice of heaven. One or two murders a year on the Kona side of the island was typical, but this was the fourth one in a month. Someone was out to solve the island's homeless problem—one murder at a time.

I continued to read the paper and sip my coffee. I don't know why, but coffee always seemed to taste better on Sunday.

Unfortunately, the news wasn't better. Story after story

of nothing but bad news and bad things that happened to good people. I sighed and muttered to myself, "Something's got to change." After a while, I folded the paper and threw it down in disgust.

It's usually quiet out at the harbor. That's why I lived there on a boat named the *Holo-Holo*. It's the perfect home for a sworn bachelor. And forty-two feet of Cabo fishing yacht nirvana. It used to be named the *Hui-Hou*. I changed it because I hated saying goodbye and because holo-holo meant cruising or vacation in Hawaiian; it was more in line with how I liked to spend my time.

Most apartments weren't as nice inside. What I liked most about it was if I got sick of the neighbors, I could untie and move to a different harbor or island if I chose to. I had no desire to, but I enjoyed having options. Living in the same house in the same neighborhood for twenty years was not my idea of living anymore.

Later that afternoon, Kathy dropped by to work on her book while I laid on the couch and studied the weather report from Kona to Honolulu. I had business over there that would take about a month, and I wanted to avoid staying in a hotel for that length of time.

It would've been a nice occasion to exercise the *Holo-Holo*, since it wasn't good to let 800 horsepower diesel engines sit idle for long periods of time.

Kathy sat at the table across from the couch. Her right hand appeared to be permanently attached to her forehead as she leaned forward with her elbow on the table. She was on the third rewrite of her first novel.

According to her, it's a love story that happened on the high seas. She said my boat was the only place she could write it because it was on water and she needed to feel a connection to the ocean to make her words authentic–whatever that meant.

When she wasn't working at the Ugly Omelette, I used her part-time when I had a charter. Fish shivered at the mere mention of her name. That's how good she was with a fishing pole.

Kathy had a red hibiscus flower in her long black hair. It was tied up into a messy bun with tendrils that streaked down the side of her face. She wore a teal bikini top with white denim shorts that contrasted her golden brown skin. She traded off chewing her hair and a pencil intermittently as she regarded the paper version of her manuscript.

The stack of pages was a sea of red and blue ink over, under, and around the printed words. If there was one thing she'd convinced me of, it was that I never wanted to be a writer; especially not after watching her write and rewrite the same story over a period of months.

I'd never been the type to sit in front of a computer for hours at a time and would definitely have thrown it overboard after the first hour. Never mind the fact that I'd sit in the boat's fighting chair with a fishing line in the water, drink beer for hours, and stare at the ocean with nothing to show for it. I wish I was a better angler. To each his own, I guess. W. C. Fields once said, "Everyone's got to believe in something, and I believe I'll have another beer." It worked for him, it worked for me.

I didn't mind Kathy coming over to write, since her perfume always improved the smell of the place.

"Crap!" she said as she stared at the manuscript.

I looked over and said, "Problem?"

"I have a plot hole big enough to drive a boat through."

I watched for a moment as she spit her hair out from between her front teeth and started scribbling wildly in the margins on the paper in front of her. The more she wrote, the more unwrinkled her face got. I nodded and went back to reading the weather report, since I wanted to avoid crossing the channel between the Big Island and Maui in twenty-foot seas.

When I saw that three tropical storms had formed off Baja, Mexico, and were headed straight toward Hawaii, it was a straightforward decision to postpone my trip to Honolulu until after hurricane season.

I was about to tell Kathy when a loud woman's voice out on the dock disrupted the evening silence. It was one of the drawbacks of not having a doorbell.

"Kathy, are you in there?"

Startled, Kathy said, "I'm sorry Jack, I told her not to come here. I'll get rid of her."

"No worries, she's fine. There will come a day when you'll miss her interrupting you. Trust me."

Kathy bounced from the table out the salon door toward the dock.

"Mom! I told you not to come here," she whispered so as not to draw the eyes of any nearby boat dwellers.

"I know honey, I'm sorry and just afraid of what I found in the backyard, and I remembered your friend Jack being in law enforcement, and–"

Kathy interrupted, "He's retired. What did you find that is so important?"

Her mother looked down the dock and at the two boats on each side of the *Holo-Holo* and whispered, "Bones."

Now really annoyed because her mother had interrupted her writing, Kathy said in a low tone of voice, "They're probably from some animal."

Her mother shook her head. "That's what I thought

until I found the skull," she said as she pulled it out of her oversized purse.

"Oh my gosh, put that back and come with me," Kathy whisper yelled as she checked to see if anyone was looking as she pulled her mother by the arm down from the dock onto the boat.

____

CHAPTER TWO

Kathy brought her mother inside the cabin of the *Holo-Holo*, almost as if she were escorting a prisoner, and presented her to me. "This is my mother, Estelle Medeiros."

My first impression was she could have been Kathy's older sister. Since Kathy was thirty-five, I'd guess Estelle was near my age. Unlike me, she didn't look it. Kathy, obviously not a good judge of age, thought I was in my mid-forties, so my ego was living the dream. My body—not so much, after a career in law enforcement and just over five decades of abuse.

I stood and reached for Estelle's hand before she sat next to Kathy on the couch. I said, "It's a pleasure to meet you. The other day, Kathy told me you're selling your house and moving back to the mainland."

Estelle smiled and nodded. "That's right, I just can't afford to live here anymore. Well, I could if I continued to work two jobs. When I was younger, it was okay, but now I just want to work less and play more. Working the rest of my life just to make ends meet is what's on the horizon if I stay here. Besides, nobody stays in Hawaii forever, except the locals. And I'd argue that with a hundred thousand Hawaiians living in Las Vegas, it's a crap shoot even for them. And don't get me started on the crime here nowadays. I read in the paper a jogger found another poor man murdered in the village this morning. It's almost like somebody has a vendetta against the homeless. Not to mention the reason I'm here."

Kathy interrupted, clearly eager to get back to working on her book. "Mom, show him the skull."

I expected several things Kathy could have said, but show him the skull wasn't on the list.

Estelle pulled it from her purse and said, "I found it in the backyard while digging up a leaky irrigation line."

In a nanosecond, I evaluated the pain-in-the-ass factor of the skull in my life and smiled as I said, "You should take it to the police station. I'm sure they would be fascinated as to how it got buried on your property."

Kathy frowned, "Jack," she whined. "I was hoping you could take care of this so my mom doesn't wind up getting thrown in jail."

Before I could say a word, Estelle blurted, "I don't want to go to the police because my house is in escrow and this skull could blow up the deal. Isn't there another way, Jack?"

"I suppose you could put it back where you found it and don't tell a soul. Besides, there are bones all over this island. It could be an ancient Hawaiian burial for all we know. Or not, let your conscience be your guide."

Estelle half smiled and nodded. She quickly put the skull back in her purse. I sensed she was annoyed that I wasn't willing to get involved. I viewed the skull as an OPM, which meant, "Other person's monkey." And had better things to do than go play twenty questions with the cops about it. Once upon a time, when I was still interested in saving the world, I would have gotten knee-deep in it. But that bus has left the station, and I'm not on it.

As she got up to leave, Estelle leaned over and hugged Kathy. She said to me, "Thanks for your time, Jack." I nodded and smiled as I waved goodbye. I could feel the burning glare from Kathy. Clearly, she was unhappy with me.

One hour later, my phone rang. I glanced at the name and muttered, "why me?" The Caller ID said it was detective Grady O'Halloran of the Kona PD. I'd known Grady a long time. We worked a few investigations together in Honolulu back in the day.

I was semi-retired, and he wasn't. There was probably some lingering resentment because I was sitting on my boat drinking beer at my leisure, and he was still working for the man.

In a gruff tone, he said, "What's the story on the skull?" Obviously, he wasn't happy about having his Sunday evening interrupted since he was the detective on call that night.

"I don't know anything about it. I told her to take it to the police station since I didn't want to be involved. If I'd known you were the one to catch the case, I would have told her to just bury it in the backyard. Who peed on your Cheerios?"

Grady sighed, "The judge. I went to court on Friday and my ex-wife got her alimony increased. I have to pay that bitch to sit on her fat ass over in Honolulu while I'm practically living in a coffee shack."

I didn't need to remind him that his stripper girlfriend in Waikiki was what caused the alimony in the first place. So, I thought I'd lighten the subject and said, "From what

I've read in the paper, it looks like there's a serial killer working this side of the island."

"That's why I'm calling you about the skull. I'm trying to figure out if this is related. Maybe the guy has been at this a long time and now is just too lazy to bury the bodies."

I changed the subject to fishing and said, "I need to get ready for a charter tomorrow."

I went fishing the next day, and Grady went to dig up Estelle's backyard.

CHAPTER THREE

On mornings when I didn't have an early charter, I liked to drink coffee while I sat out on the rocky point at the mouth of the harbor. More often than not, I had a front-row seat when a pod of dolphins cruised by. Occasionally, my coffee drinking buddy Miles was already there when I showed up.

He was easy to spot with his long reddish-blonde dreadlocks. He never wore a shirt. His skin looked like tanned leather from years of exposure to the Hawaiian sun. Near his left shoulder was a scar from a bullet wound. I knew what it was when I first saw it because I had one similar to it. I asked him about it once. He said he got it in Vietnam on hill 488 just south of Chu Lai, courtesy of the Viet Cong. I lifted my shirt and showed him the one I got in Somalia.

Anyone who had ever met him would've never forgotten his piercing blue eyes. If I were to guess, I'd say his heritage was Scandinavian, and at the time he was in his late sixties or early seventies. The lines on his face said life had been tough, but you'd never have known it by talking with him.

From all outward appearances, he had little in the way

of material things, but he seemed to be one of the happiest people I knew. I wished I had his guts to just say screw it and go live on the beach like he did.

I'd wear a fishhook necklace like he had and just live off the land. But I couldn't end my lifelong relationship with hot water and soap. Thus, I was a slave to the man, just like everyone else that lived indoors.

Usually Miles arrived before me when he'd camped out in the Honokohau National Park next to the harbor. He had other places around the island he liked to stay, but he said the park was his favorite. The park rangers and he play a game similar to whack a mole. He was easy to spot because of his rat dog, Pierre. He always barked at the rangers when they were making their rounds, regardless of how many times Miles shushed him to be quiet.

Pierre had short brown fur and was only about eight inches tall and a foot long. He wasn't prejudiced; he hated everybody except Miles. I suspected he tolerated me only because I brought him treats as a bribe to keep from getting bit. He acted like he was every bit as big and tough as any German Shepherd.

When the rangers found Miles and Pierre sleeping in one spot, they just moved to another campsite the next night. They were the least of the rangers' problems.

The rangers' number one problem was a Hawaiian Ohana that lived on the beach near the canoe shed. They'd made a federal case out of the right to live in the park. According to statements they'd made to the press, they weren't moving anytime soon.

As Miles and I watched the fishing boats leave the harbor headed toward the fishing grounds, he took a sip of coffee and said, "The rangers are serious this time, Jack. It's not like the old days. Pierre and I have to move into town."

"Well, you guys had a good run. You probably could've stayed a few more years if it weren't for your little friend's pleasant personality." I cut my eyes toward Pierre. He was too busy gnawing on his milk bone to care about my sarcasm. "How long have you lived there, five years?"

Miles nodded. "Something like that."

"Well, I guess we can start having coffee down at The Ugly Omelette."

"You don't have to do that, Jack."

I smiled and teased, "How else are we going to solve all the world's problems while we have coffee? And besides, canoe racing starts soon. We can watch all the scantily clad wahines practice, and who knows, you might even find yourself a new girlfriend down there."

Miles grimaced. "No more girlfriends. It's just me and Pierre from now on."

I nodded. "I understand where you're coming from. I've been married three times, and have no desire for love to lie to me again."

After a sip of coffee, I added, "You might think about checking into the shelter for a while."

He shook his head, "No can, they won't allow Pierre. We'll just sleep on the beach at Honl's."

Usually, Miles and I would stare at the ocean while we talked and drank coffee. I shifted my body toward him and looked him in the eye, so he would see I was serious, and said, "There's something going on in the village, and it's not safe there at night."

"You mean the four dead people found during the last month?"

"Yeah, that's precisely what I mean."

Miles smiled as he reached over and scratched behind

Pierre's ear as he looked down toward the poi dog. "No worries, he's got my back. Just ask the rangers."

I took the last sip of my coffee and said, "Just be careful," as I stood up to leave. Miles nodded and looked back toward the ocean.

While I walked back to the *Holo-Holo,* I couldn't help but wonder about the skull Estelle had found. Was it related to the murders, or was it really from an ancient burial site? I fought the urge to call Grady all the way back to the boat.

CHAPTER FOUR

I arrived at The Ugly Omelette and took my usual table off to the side where I could sit with my back against the wall. It had a marvelous view of Kailua bay. The place bustled with the sound of plates clattering and the smell of bacon and eggs in the air. They specialized in omelets, but I lived for their banana pancakes with a side of bacon.

The place was a hole in the wall and had quickly become the place to go for breakfast since it opened earlier in the year. Starting a restaurant wasn't for the weak at heart. In Hawaii, double that factor because of shipping fees and finding employees. I could recall three different places that were there before. They didn't make it for one reason or another.

It was an open air joint on the second floor with a view. I loved being able to watch all the activities that went on in Kailua Bay while I ate. The start and finish line of the canoe races was visible from almost every chair in the place.

It had a sixty's surfer vibe because of all the old surfboards that hung from the ceiling. Though the place was small, the food was outstanding. The last three restaurants that set out to make a go of it there didn't make it because their food sucked.

Everybody in town always tried the new place the first couple of months they were open. If the food was no good, they were toast because word traveled fast around town.

The Ugly Omelette had a small crew, four waitresses and the chef, Jeff. He was the executive chef at one of the resorts on the Kohala coast who'd tired of the corporate world and decided to open his own restaurant in town. He and the crew treated you like family. They remembered my name when I came in. It was where I met Kathy. She worked part time. Eventually, I hired her to help me on the boat. It turned out she had mad fishing skills besides being an aspiring writer. She reminded me a lot of my daughter, who I missed so much.

Kathy gave me the cold shoulder for the most part that morning. Usually, when she took my order, she was very chatty, but since I hadn't run to her mother's rescue, she'd decided to punish me.

Other than "The usual?" the only other thing she said was the cops were over digging up her mother's yard and her mother, Estelle, was freaked out.

It was against my better judgment, but when she brought my omelet, I said, "I'll make a phone call after I eat and see what I can find out about the skull. It's going to be limited information since I'm not on the job anymore, but I'll see what I can do."

Once I retired, I became a private citizen and that cut me off from most of the information in an active investigation. That's just how it was, which was fine because, like I said, I preferred not to get involved. But since Kathy had become like family, I had to see what I could do if I didn't want her to spit in my eggs.

About that time, Miles showed up and joined me. Pierre laid on the floor at his feet. He probably wasn't allowed there either, but nobody said anything since he was pretty small and out of sight under the table most of the time. He was a smart dog and well-behaved in public when he wanted to be. I thought it was mainly the park rangers waking him up that pissed him off . I considered offering Miles a temporary home for Pierre, so Miles could check into the shelter, but I knew he wouldn't have any part of that.

Kathy saw Miles sit down and brought a cup of coffee over and smiled. He was a funny guy. When you saw him, you knew he was homeless. There was no misunderstanding about his hygiene program. It was clear he didn't have one. He had a layer of dirt on him that probably worked as an armored suit against the elements, one could argue. I just made sure I sat up wind when we had coffee together. But the thing was, he was personable, and people liked to talk with him, and he them. I had seen him at various eateries up and down Ali'i Drive, having coffee and chatting with folks all the time.

I felt my phone vibrate in my shirt pocket. I tilted it out just far enough to see the caller ID, and it was Grady. That was great, since it'd saved me from having to call him. I answered, "What's up?"

"Estelle didn't mention she'd found that skull in a lava tube, did she?" Grady asked.

"No, but then again, I didn't ask her any questions about it because I preferred not to know anything."

"Well, the good news is it looks like an ancient burial site. I'll contact the burial council and they'll relocate the bones, and everybody will be happy at the end of this deal."

I got off the phone with Grady just as Kathy came over to warm up my coffee and bring Miles his toast.

"Good news. Your mother's going to be able to close escrow. I just got off the phone with the detective handling her case. He said the skull is from an ancient burial, so there will not be any further investigation."

Kathy's face lit up. "I knew you would come through, Jack. I'll call my mom and let her know she can quit freaking out—and I'll see you on the boat as soon as my shift is over."

CHAPTER FIVE

After breakfast, I'd gone back to the boat to wait for Kathy and my half-day charter to arrive. She had an hour left on her shift, and once she and the client were onboard, we'd get underway. Lately, the fish hadn't been biting, and having Kathy as my first mate was an excellent distraction from the lack of fishing action. When you charge four hundred and fifty bucks for a half-day charter and there are no fish to catch, you have to be very entertaining. If the client doesn't catch any fish, Kathy teases them like they're going on a date after the charter is over. Most of my clients are old rich guys, and they fall for it almost every time, except for one guy named Jerry. He's gay and owns a couple of strip clubs in Vegas and, as luck would have it, he's the one we're taking fishing today.

While I waited for them, I killed time and read the morning paper. I read with amusement about a real estate developer named Aldrich Cook. For over a year, he's attempted to sell a large commercial project for ten million dollars.

According to the article, he was fed up with the homeless blowing up his deal. Time after time, buyers backed out because of what they perceived as riffraff hanging around the front of the building. The article also quoted Cook saying everything was great until the buyer arrived from the mainland and saw all the tents up on the sidewalk next to his building. He said he's complained to the county, and it'd fallen on deaf ears.

With all the development going on, it wouldn't be long before Kona looked like Honolulu with commercial buildings. When it did, or the crime got worse, I'd have to go find a new island to live on. I thought maybe I should've checked out New Zealand, since it was where a lot of people from Hawaii would go on vacation. But for an American to get a permanent visa to live there, I heard it would take a million dollars cash. I'd probably have to move to Las Vegas instead. It's what a lot of locals consider the ninth island. Over a hundred thousand Hawaiians had made the move. I thought that would most likely be where I'd wind up.

The paper ran an article recently that said Cook would soon put money up for a homeless shelter. Most likely, he's trying to get them off the sidewalk in front of his building and out of sight. He's become the darling of various local charities. It seems like every time I opened the newspaper I saw his face on the front page. Usually, it was with some kind of promotion, chipping away at what is left of the undeveloped part of the island. Since I have a job in Vegas next week, I should probably look at property there for when the day comes I've had enough and have decided to move.

Some peripheral movement caught my attention. I looked up from the paper and glanced down the dock, and saw Jerry on his way toward the boat. I looked at my watch and saw he was right on time. What was unusual was Kathy had not shown up yet. I figured she got stuck in traffic and was on her way. After I got Jerry situated in the cabin with a Bloody Mary, we waited for Kathy to arrive.

Ten minutes later, she came running down the dock. As she came onboard, I asked her, "What happened?"

Almost out of breath, she followed me into the cabin and said, "That son of a bitch right there," and pointed toward the front page of the newspaper that was now lying on the table. He came in and was my next table after you'd left. My brow furrowed as I was perplexed that somehow Mr. Wonderful, according to the newspaper, was the reason she was delayed. Until she said, "Don't believe none of that shit you read in the paper about what a saint Aldrich Cook is. He's one of the biggest assholes on this island." She continued, "He makes all kinds of sexual innuendos every time I take his order, and I'm sick of it. I've politely asked him to stop twice, but that doesn't seem to faze him a bit. I told Jeff I'm going to quit if he doesn't do something about it. Jeff said he'll wait on him from now on."

Jerry was in the head and overheard Kathy. When he came out, he said, "Do you need me to have my boyfriend go tune him up for you, honey?" Kathy smiled. "Not yet, but thanks for the offer."

I was pretty sure Jerry was kidding, but before she changed her mind, I interjected, "Sounds like Jeff is handling it. Write your novel faster is the only advice I can give you. The quicker you produce a best-selling book to replace your income, the sooner you can quit that job and not have to put up with the likes of scumbags like Cook anymore." I grinned and said, "But–you can never quit this job, slaves have to be sold. Now let's go catch some fish."

CHAPTER SIX

Thank God, Jerry caught fish. I was afraid he'd want me to blow him if he hadn't. He caught a marlin. We tagged it and let it go. We brought half a dozen ono and a couple of mahi-mahis back to the harbor. Kathy and I were busy cleaning the boat. We'd already cleaned and packaged the fish for Jerry, and he'd just left.

I was up on the flybridge wiping down the controls after a freshwater rinse. I had a bird's-eye view of the harbor parking area when I saw Grady's Crown Vic pull into the lot. I thought little of it when he got out of the car until he reached in and pulled a small dog carrier out of the back seat. From where I was, I could not see what he had inside, but I could hear the barking. A sharp pang settled into my gut. I had a bad feeling about why Grady was here.

I climbed down from the flybridge to the deck as Grady walked toward the dock. Kathy was finishing up wiping down the boat and I said, "That's good enough, we're done." She looked at me funny. She probably sensed something was up by the way I'd gone from joking around earlier like we did to being quietly serious.

Kathy grabbed her bag out of the cabin and said, "I'm off to help my mom pack up her house. I'll see you later." I nodded and watched her walk past Grady on the dock and do a double take of Pierre inside the carrier.

When Grady got to the boat, he set the carrier on the dock, stepped down into the cockpit, and took a seat on the rail. I sat in the fighting chair and waited for him to say something.

"Last night there was another stabbing, and the victim was Miles Goodmunson. We found your name in his backpack as his emergency contact. It also said to bring you the dog if something happened to him. Be careful, he bites like an alligator." Grady showed me the top of his right hand that had a couple of fresh puncture wounds.

I nodded, "The secret to the dog is this," and I pulled a small treat out of my pocket. "I grabbed it out of the cabin after I saw you park. What happened to Miles?"

"He's victim number five of what we're calling the West Side Slasher."

"Was he at Honl's?"

Grady nodded and said, "The dog was lying next to him when he was found."

"Any witnesses?"

Grady shook his head.

"Miles was a good guy. He didn't deserve this–" As I spoke, the lump in my throat disappeared and the sharp pain in my gut faded. It was replaced by the heat of anger that began to build. As much as I wasn't a fan of Pierre, I felt the least I could do was honor Miles' last wish, if you want to call it that, and said, "I'll take the dog."

"Good, I didn't want to take him to the pound."

"Do you have any leads?"

"Nothing yet. We canvassed the condos next door and

across the street from the beach; nobody saw or heard anything."

After Grady left Pierre, I sat in the fighting chair, staring at the dog and him at me. It had been a long time since I had a dog on the boat, and he wasn't exactly the type of dog I would get if I were looking for one. But his one and only friend in this world was dead, and if not me, then who would take him? Miles' death was bad enough. Sending Pierre to the pound would most likely be the end of him too. I couldn't do that to him, even if he was an ornery little bastard.

I picked up the carrier from the dock and sat it next to the fighting chair in the cockpit. I wedged a dog biscuit through the bars on the door. While Pierre was busy chewing on the biscuit, I went to get a small rope to use as a leash. I had no plans to take him anywhere. I just needed to get him out of the carrier. As I was getting the line, it occurred to me that there was no way he was getting off the boat if I let him out of the carrier to run free in the cockpit. So, I spread a couple of biscuits around the deck and headed to the store to buy some real dog food.

After picking up some dog chow, I headed to Honl's beach. I wanted to see the crime scene for myself. Grady's a top-notch investigator, but it wouldn't hurt to have another set of eyes look around.

I parked on Ali'i Dr. next to the rock wall fronting Honl's. It was a four and a half mile long road that ran along the shoreline from the Kailua pier to Keauhou. It was dotted with small beaches and bungalows along the way. The view was tranquil and exotic, not exactly a place you would expect to find someone stabbed to death on the beach.

I was across from the Ali'i Cove condos. Before I got out of my truck, I watched boogie boarders ride small waves and play chicken with the reef. I did that for a few minutes while I tried to get my head in the right place. When I was on the job, I'd investigated many homicides while I ate a sandwich. Murder was a regular part of my daily life for many years. So much so that I'd become numb to it. But this was different because Miles was a good friend and practically a Kona icon.

He'd been around long before all the riffraff that had invaded the town. He wasn't a beggar; he just chose to live outdoors and bathe in the ocean once in a while. Miles marched to his own drummer. I respected that.

I should've probably sat this one out and let Grady do his investigation, but I needed to take a brief look first just to satisfy my curiosity, and to make sure he hadn't missed anything.

I stood in the sand at the south end of the beach next to the rock wall where Grady said a surfer had found Miles' body. To the left was an abandoned house. I scanned toward the condominium complex at the north end while looking for anything out of place. The beach was about a hundred yards long and a small park sat between it and Ali'i Dr. at the north end.

I walked the beach and looked for anything out of place and, not finding it, I headed back to my truck. Grady was right. There wasn't anything to go on. That was until I noticed a webcam in the window of a condo at Ali'i Cove. Grady probably saw it too, but I had to know. I called him and got his answering machine, so I left a message, "Hey Grady, it's Jack, did you see that webcam in the window of the end unit condo overlooking the beach? Call me back."

I drove home to the harbor. Kathy was coming over to work on her book. I needed to get back to the *Holo-Holo* before she arrived, so Pierre wouldn't put the bite on her.

I made good time getting to the harbor and was pretty sure I'd be there before Kathy. That was until I saw her yellow Volkswagen bug parked in the lot as I pulled in. Crap.

The last thing I expected when I walked down the dock toward the boat was Kathy sitting in the fighting chair, stroking Pierre's back while he laid on her lap with his eyes closed.

When I got onboard, I said, "What did you drug him with?"

She smiled.

"He loves me because I gave him a piece of steak. I brought it with me from my mom's house. She was cleaning out the refrigerator and gave me a bunch of stuff." Her eyebrows narrowed. "I heard about Miles. I'm sorry. Do the cops have any suspects?"

"Not yet, but that may change soon. How'd you like to take Pierre home with you? He comes with a free bag of dog food."

Kathy looked down at him while she rubbed his head and said, "My roommate has a cat, so there's no way that would work."

I nodded. "It was worth a try. I have to go call Grady and find a food bowl for Pierre."

CHAPTER SEVEN

After Kathy went home last night, Pierre and I squared off at opposite corners of the cabin. I picked the couch to lie on next to the cabin door. He laid under the table next to the galley, occasionally raising his head to give me what I interpreted as a dirty look. Both of us trying to figure out how to get rid of the other.

It was about 9:30 pm when the phone rang. It was Grady. He said, "Do you know if Miles has any family? I'm having a hard time locating any next of kin."

"No, he never talked about family. From the conversations we had, he'd pretty much sworn off women and said it was just him and Pierre."

"Did you know he was a vet and had been awarded the Navy Cross?"

"Navy Cross? No, I knew he'd gone to Vietnam and caught an AK round in the shoulder that left a gnarly scar. He had to survive some serious shit to get that medal. How did you know he was a vet?"

"In his pocket, there was a key to a storage locker over in the old industrial area. I went there looking for any information to locate his next of kin. When I opened the locker, I found a box that had the Vietnam ribbon, a Purple Heart, and the Navy Cross. His service record was also there. He was a Navy corpsman."

"It doesn't surprise me. He never said a word about it. What does is how someone was able to murder him."

"It looks like he was probably drunk. I found an empty bottle of Mad Dog 20/20 next to him in the sand. When the toxicology report comes back, I won't be surprised if he wasn't pickled."

"I know Miles liked to crawl into the bottle from time to time. After you dropped the dog off, I went over to Honl's to have a look around. Did you see the webcam in the window of the end unit at the south end of Ali'i Cove?"

"I did. I went over and knocked on the door and talked to the guy that lives there. He said that it's broken and has been for months."

After I got off the phone with Grady, I thought about Miles, and how he didn't deserve what had happened to him. Especially after the raw deal that vets like him got after coming back from Vietnam. Miles' killer needed to pay for it, and not with a life sentence. He needed to pay with a life —his life.

As much as I didn't want to investigate another murder, this was different. I had a duty to Miles as a fellow vet, and because he deserved justice.

I glanced over at Pierre. He had gone to sleep. It looked like a good idea to me and I closed my eyes, but I kept thinking about the broken webcam in the window. I was almost asleep when I was jolted awake by the thought there might be another one overlooking the beach, and we just hadn't seen it. I sat up, grabbed my laptop, and started looking for webcams along Ali'i Dr.

It took a while, but I found one pointed north toward the direction of the beach where the murder happened. Of course, there wasn't an address on the website of the physical location of the camera. The next morning I'd head back to Honl's to look for it.

I glanced at Pierre when I noticed him fidgeting in his sleep. I didn't doubt he was having a nightmare. My first thought was poor little guy, and to stroke him like Kathy had. Then the rational part of my brain took over and reminded me it probably wouldn't end well for me if I did, so I said quietly, "Don't you worry, I'll find the bastard who took Miles from us and feed him to the sharks."

CHAPTER EIGHT

After I got up, the first two things I did were cancel my business trip to Vegas, and all charters for the time being.

After I took Pierre out to handle his morning business, I went down to The Ugly Omelette to get coffee and let Kathy know I wouldn't need her for a few days.

As much as I didn't want to, I brought Pierre with me. Normally, I would've just left him outside in the cockpit, but it was raining hard, and I didn't want to do that to the little guy. I also didn't want to leave him inside the cabin by himself. My new custom leather couch wasn't going to be his new chew toy. Therefore, he would come with me from now on when I left the *Holo-Holo* if it was raining.

I sat at my usual table, and Pierre laid underneath like he always had with Miles. Kathy was busy waiting tables, but noticed us and brought coffee and a treat for Pierre. Apparently, she kept a box of doggie biscuits in the kitchen for him. Again, I wondered if maybe she would like to take permanent custody of the miniature alligator. Then I remembered what she'd said about her roommate having a cat.

I scanned the morning paper as Kathy set my coffee down on the table. I noticed a bruise on her arm just above the elbow, which made me look up at her face. Her black eye that she'd tried to cover with makeup told me everything I needed to know.

She said, "You want the special? It's fresh Ahi."

I frowned and said, "What happened there?" as I stared and jutted my chin toward her bruises.

"Oh, it's nothing."

"Honey, nothing doesn't leave bruises."

There was more to the story than she was telling. I wanted to ask her to tell me the truth. But it wasn't the time, or place, and the last thing I wanted to do was upset her while she was at work.

I'd dealt with countless expert liars in my lifetime, but Kathy wasn't one of them.

I looked away toward the cruise ship in the bay and said, "I'll just have coffee." Not wanting her to see my eyes become watery at the thought of someone doing harm to her, I swallowed and blinked, willing the tears away before they could give me away.

The thought of food made me nauseous. Since Miles' murder, I hadn't felt like eating. I gave Kathy the news about canceling our charters and told her I had a lead to go run down. I said, "I'll see you at the boat tonight," as I glanced again at the bruise on her arm for a moment. She looked me right in the eye and said, "It's nothing, really." I knew better, but nodded anyway.

I'd left my truck in the parking lot at the King Kam hotel and walked to Honl's, since the sky had cleared for the time being. I figured Pierre and I could use the exercise.

The village was alive as hundreds of birds announced another day while we walked by the large Banyan tree next to the Hulihe'e Palace. Their chatter drowned out the sound of the light surf slapping against the sea wall.

The other thing I noticed as we strolled Ali'i Drive was an overwhelming number of homeless people. A phenomenon that bothered me a great deal.

My first inclination was I thought they needed to suck it up and fix their lives. But the more I looked at the situation, the more I realized it wasn't always their fault. Many of them were the result of an economic world they had no control over, and they were the collateral damage.

Instead of condemning them, we had to help them. I pondered. The ones that truly needed help, that was. Not the faction of them that had mooched off the system as a way of life and had no interest in being helped. For those people, I had zero compassion and would loved to put them on a plane back to the mainland where they'd come from.

By the time I reached Honl's, I'd solved all the world's problems in my head. I missed the philosophical discussions I used to have with Miles. It just wasn't the same without him.

As I walked along the shoreline, I realized why Grady missed the webcam. I was at the north end of the beach, looking toward the condo units. I was certain the webcam hung from under the eve of the corner unit, facing me. Because when I looked behind me down the beach that was undoubtedly the view I saw on my laptop the night before. When I looked up at the corner unit, the only thing I saw were two sunscreens pulled down. One screen in the front and one on the side facing the beach. Most likely, they were blocking my view of the camera. That explained why Grady hadn't seen it the other day.

I knocked on the front door of the condo. A man named Scott Brown answered. My hypothesis was correct. He said he pulled down the sunscreens in the mornings because the last few days there were cruise ships anchored out a couple of hundred yards in front of his place. He didn't enjoy having two thousand people stare into the double sliding glass doors of his living room every morning. Then he put them up just before he left for work.

According to Brown, the webcam video wasn't saved to a hard drive, so there was no recording of the murder. He said the video feed I saw the night before was embedded on his website so he could make a few bucks from advertising.

It was another dead end, then it occurred to me as I walked back to the village. What if somebody actually watched the live video at the time of the murder? I went back to Brown's condo and asked him if he would announce a reward on his website. He said he'd be glad to.

I had little hope of that actually working as I drove back to the harbor. When I got back to the *Holo-Holo* I felt restless and took Pierre to the mouth of the harbor to sit on the rocks and stare at the ocean for a while.

After a few minutes of watching a pod of dolphins cruise by, my mind had become quiet. The endless chatter that usually occupied it was gone, and I knew exactly what I had to do. Grady would not like it, but I knew it had to be done to find the killer.

CHAPTER NINE

I was right. Grady didn't like it when I gave him a heads-up the next morning, but he couldn't do anything about it since I didn't work for him. Dressing the part for the undercover operation would be easy, since I had a closet full of old ragged clothes in storage that I should've thrown away years ago.

After I texted Grady, I went to see Kathy at The Ugly Omelette. She'd worn a long sleeve shirt, so I could not see the bruise on her arm. She still had swelling around her eye that no amount of makeup would hide.

After she brought my coffee, I lied and said, "I have to go to Hilo on business, here's a key to the boat, make yourself comfortable while I'm gone. There's plenty of food for you and Pierre in the galley. His is under the sink."

"When will you be back?"

"I don't know. It could be days or weeks." I handed her a hundred dollar bill and said, "This should take care of the dog food if you run out. I'll pay you for your time when I get back. Oh, one more thing, that nothing that caused your bruises, I'll deal with when I get back. Stay on the boat, and you'll be safe there."

Kathy shook her head. "No need."

I frowned. "We'll talk about it when I return."

After I left the restaurant, I went to my storage unit to get dressed.

I had an old military issue blanket that would make a great shawl I could wear over my head as a disguise, so I wouldn't be easily recognized by anybody that knew me. It would be perfect for the job since nighttime temps had cooled off.

Wintertime in Hawaii could be downright nippy in the early morning hours when you're used to eighty-plus degree days. It was mid-January, and snow covered the top half of Mauna Kea. The chilly wind that blew over the mountain and down into town reminded me why I lived on a boat, as far away from the snow as I could get.

My home during the operation would be my storage unit. I had set up a cot there to sleep on during the day. Nights I would spend on the beach pretending to be asleep. The first couple of weeks my plan was to spend the night at Honl's beach. I hoped the killer would return. It was a long shot. I tried to make it appear I'd set up camp on the beach to see if that would draw him out.

For almost two weeks it was crickets, except for a couple of locals who tried to roll me. Nothing like a gun in the face to convince them otherwise. Other than that, camping on the beach brought back memories of growing up on the island and camping along the shoreline.

There's nothing like lying in a sleeping bag listening to the waves at night while staring at the millions of stars overhead. I wondered why I hadn't done that in the last fifteen or twenty years.

It was a Friday night, at about 2 a.m., and I had seriously thought of ending the stakeout at Honl's and moving to another location.

I'd just about decided when a dark outline of a man caught my attention. He was headed toward me from the north end of the beach. I was on my side with my back against the rock retaining wall that butted up against Ali'i Drive. The wall separated the beach from the road and formed a nook where I'd positioned myself. From the killer's perspective, I was a perfect target since I was cornered and out of view from people that might pass by on the road above.

I acted as if I was asleep as the shadowy figure approached. There was a large empty vodka bottle that glistened in the moonlight, lying next to me to make it look like I'd passed out drunk.

As much as I wanted to pull my Glock before he got any closer, I wanted a conviction, and the only way that would happen was by letting the murderer attack me. Catching him with just a knife would not be enough. Maybe I'd be lucky and get to kill the guy. Or perhaps I wouldn't be so lucky, and he stabs me in the throat, and I die right there.

My heart rate skyrocketed as the adrenaline pumped harder through my body. I began combat breathing, a technique a Navy SEAL buddy taught me to get settled down when in the "middle of the shit," as he liked to say.

It was like slow motion when the attacker was upon me. He pulled a dagger and thrust it into my mid-section in a burst of what he probably thought would surely kill me. His speed and ferocity were like that of a shark going after helpless prey. A prison hit with a shiv would have been less violent.

What he didn't know was the blade wasn't going through my vest, hidden under my blanket. I had the evidence I needed and had played human pin cushion long enough. I pushed him away and pulled my Glock before he shoved the dagger somewhere not covered by the vest. I grabbed the Glock lying next to me on the blanket, aimed, and squeezed the trigger. The round hit him in the shoulder. The force of the bullet spun him away from me. It knocked him down face-first into the sand. He tried to get up and run, but I'd quickly pounced on top of him.

I pressed my knee into his shoulder that had the bullet in it. I pulled his arms together behind his back to cuff him as he cried out in pain. "Good, I'm glad it hurts, you piece of shit. You're lucky I don't put one in the back of your skull. The world would be better off without you."

"Just let me go. I can pay," he whined.

"You're going to pay, all right. I don't want your money; I want your life."

"Please don't kill me—Please!"

He must have sensed how easy it would've been for me to take my vest off and use it to muffle the sound of a gunshot. Miles was a good friend. Had he been a family member, I probably would've pulled the trigger. But I wasn't willing to risk prison, even though the Westside Slasher deserved to be put down like a rabid animal.

Hawaii didn't have a death penalty, and if there was ever a man who deserved it, it was this guy. As much as I didn't want to, I applied hemostatic gauze to the bullet hole to stop the bleeding before I called the cops.

Since it was after the bars had closed, the Kona PD arrived in less than three minutes after I'd called 911. It was a good thing I'd set up a trail camera to document the attack because the killer wasn't whom I expected to see coming at me with a dagger. But there he stood, spewing his version of how he was the victim to the arriving officers.

They weren't exactly in a rush to take a pillar of the community off to jail until I played the video from the trail cam that showed him trying to kill me. Now it was up to Grady and the deputy district attorney to put Aldrich Cook in prison for life.

CHAPTER TEN

I'd gone back to the *Holo-Holo* to take a shower and get some shut-eye in a proper bed. When the phone rang, I was almost asleep. I picked it up and squinted at the small screen without my reading glasses. All I saw was a long blur of text. I guessed it was probably Grady. I tapped the screen to answer.

Luckily, I'd guessed right, and it wasn't a telemarketer. Grady said, "The deputy DA says there's not enough evidence to charge Aldrich Cook for any of the murders. We don't have any DNA or witnesses. Like I told you before, I wasn't holding anything back. The good news is he's willing to charge Cook with first-degree attempted murder in your case, since there's video. Cook's looking at life without parole, and that will give us time to look for a witness in one of the other cases."

I nodded while I held the phone to my ear and said, "There's no doubt in my mind he's the guy responsible. It only makes sense for him to target the homeless. He's on record in the newspaper blaming them for repeatedly blowing up the sale of his commercial building. He's had it on the market a long time, according to the article I read."

"I don't disagree. We just don't have any evidence that he's the Westside Slayer. Find me a witness to one of the murders, and I think the deputy DA will be happy to charge him."

"After I get some sleep, I'll see what I can do."

I hung up the phone and thought about the reward offered. There had only been a couple of leads, and they had gone nowhere. It was time to increase the reward. In some investigations I'd worked on when I was on the job, nothing made the phone ring like a big reward. I would definitely post Grady's phone number instead of mine, since a big reward would also bring out all the nut jobs.

I wanted to raise the reward to a hundred grand. But since I didn't have another seventy-five thousand to add to the twenty-five thousand that I'd already put up, I'd have to make a phone call to raise it, after I'd gotten some sleep. It didn't take me long to doze off, and I slept well for the first time since Miles' murder. I didn't awake until just after noon, when I heard Kathy banging around in the galley.

"You're moving pretty slow there, old man," Kathy said as I came up the steps from my stateroom into the galley. I nodded, but didn't mention Cook tried to stick a dagger through me a half a dozen times. Though his dagger hadn't gone through my vest, I definitely was sore from the pounding I'd gotten from Cook's multiple attempts to turn my guts into sashimi.

I was thirsty and momentarily couldn't decide on coffee or beer. Coffee I had to make and wait for, beer was in the refrigerator. Beer it was while I waited on the coffee to brew. I took a seat at the table next to the galley. I looked at the beer can in front of me and thought about the fact that I'd been sober twenty-four-seven the last two weeks, and wondered for a moment if maybe I should continue the streak for a while. I didn't plan to quit drinking; perhaps just extend the timeout I'd taken to hunt for Miles' killer.

There was enough to fill a cup when I looked at the coffeepot. I grabbed the beer can off the table, got up, put it back in the refrigerator, and poured a cup of coffee, then sat back down at the table. I looked at the cup and said, "Don't make me regret this," just before I took a sip.

After my taste buds savored the first sip, I glanced at Kathy and didn't see any bruises. With her eyes focused on her laptop computer screen, she hadn't noticed me checking her over.

She'd moved to the couch from the galley, and sat with her legs crossed in the lotus position. My knees hurt just looking at her. Pierre had tucked himself in close to her on the side furthest away from me. Her fingers were a blur as she typed words into her manuscript.

When she paused for a minute, I said, "It looks like you got that plot hole figured out." She smiled and said, "The story's coming along fine. My heroine is falling in love with an older man."

I smiled and nodded. "Tell me about those bruises you had a couple of weeks ago."

I'd clearly knocked her out of her happy place by the look on her face. She shook her head and, with a furrowed brow, said, "He won't do it again. He promised."

I nodded, then took a sip of coffee while I chose my words carefully.

"That's what they always say. What's his name and where do I find him?"

"You don't have to say anything to him. Besides, he's dangerous."

"Oh, but I do. Let's just say he's going to have a come-to-Jesus moment—what's his name?"

Kathy's brow wrinkled again. It was clear she preferred not to name the perpetrator, but she could see I would not let it go, and finally said, "Larry Johnson."

"What rock does Larry Johnson hide under?"

"You can probably find him at Banyan's most mornings. He has a yellow surfboard with a big red lightning bolt. If the surf is up, he'll be there for sure."

"I take it he's an old boyfriend?"

Kathy nodded. "We broke up a long time ago because, among other things, he was a controlling asshole. I hadn't seen him in three years because he'd gone to prison for possession of a stolen rifle. It was right after I told him I never wanted to see him again. I was at Walmart a few weeks ago when he saw me walk out of the store. He followed me to my car. He said he'd just gotten released and wanted us to get back together. I told him no thanks. When I went to get into my car, he grabbed my arm and jerked me toward him. That's how I got that bruise. I slapped him, and he slugged me in the eye. He let go after I pepper sprayed his ass. I doubt he wants more of that in the future."

"Good girl–but I still need to have a chat with him. Does he have any moles, tats, scars, or other distinguishing features? Haole boy or local?"

"He's kama'aina. You can't miss the tat on the side of his neck of the Big Island. He's also got a tribal band on his left arm above the elbow. Be careful, he did a lot of MMA fighting here and on the Hilo side. He never lost a fight in the ring, and probably could've made it to the big time up in Vegas if he hadn't gone to jail. I wouldn't want him to put dirty lickin's on you. That's why I don't want you to say anything to him."

I smiled and nodded. "Thanks for the heads-up. I'll be careful. Oh, one more thing, you don't have to worry about Aldrich Cook harassing you at work anymore. Long story short, he's going to prison for attempted murder. You can read about it in tomorrow's paper."

Kathy froze, her mouth hung open for a long moment before she said, "I knew he was a creep, but I had no idea. I can't wait to read about it, but first I have to finish the book."

CHAPTER ELEVEN

Two days later.

To increase the reward to seventy-five grand, I needed to call the richest guy I knew, Sam Stuart. I'd called him two days earlier but hadn't gotten an answer.

He was in the yacht building business and had done well. He had more money than your typical billionaire and married my niece Jessica a year earlier. I doubted that would have any weight in his decision to pony up the cash, but I'd hoped so.

I hated asking people for money, and as a rule, never would. But this was different. I needed a witness to Miles' or any of the other murders. Raising the reward was the only play I had left.

That evening, I dialed Sam. He picked up on the first ring. "Hey Sam, it's Jack. I won't bore you with pleasantries. I need seventy-five grand." I expected him to say something like, "Yeah, people in Hell need ice water." But he didn't. Since he didn't hang up on me right away, I continued, "I don't know if you're familiar with the murder case of Miles Goodmunson. I've put up a reward of twenty-five thousand but have gotten no response. The only thing left to do is increase the reward. That's why I need the money."

Sam didn't miss a beat. "That's what I like about you, Jack. No bullshit, right to the point. Why is Miles' case so important to you? I thought you were retired?"

"Miles was a Vietnam vet, and a highly decorated Navy corpsman. He'd served his country and gotten very little in return. He gave more than he got in life, and that's why I care."

"I agree, Jack. I knew Miles, though not very well. I'd run across him in the village and spoke with him a time or two. I met him when he was selling palm frond hats that he'd woven as he sat there watching the tourists walk by. I was impressed by his entrepreneurial spirit. His spot was on the rock wall next to the pier. He was a good guy. I'd be happy to add a hundred thousand to the reward."

I was stunned. I didn't expect it to be that easy and get that much. It shouldn't have surprised me. I'd seen Sam generously donate to many island causes over the last couple of years.

"Thanks Sam, I really appreciate it. If a witness comes forward, and you wind up paying the reward, I'll be happy to take you fishing for the rest of your life."

Sam laughed. "You know I own a boat, right?"

"I know, but you don't have me. I know where all the secret spots are that the marlin like to hang out." We both laughed and promised to get together and talk story sooner than later.

Sam was gracious and made it easy, but I still hated to ask him for the money.

. . .

It was o-dark thirty when I paddled out of the harbor. It felt good to be back on my one-man canoe. I followed a Hatteras out and drafted in its wake until we reached the buoy outside the mouth of the harbor. It sped up toward the fishing grounds and quickly left me behind.

I turned the canoe south toward Banyans and set a moderate pace. The sea was calm, and the moon was bright. There wasn't any wind. I dug deep with my paddle when I noticed a couple of dolphins alongside. Keeping up with them wasn't going to happen. "Show-offs," I said as they pulled away. I'd felt good about my pace until they'd come along. Compared to them, it was as if I were going backwards. Good thing I left early.

The sky shifted from darkness to twilight, and I picked up the pace. The more light I saw behind Mt. Hualalai, the quicker I paddled. I wanted to be at Banyans before the first surfers paddled out.

As I approached the beach, I saw two surfers who had already made it out beyond the surf break. Neither of them had a neck tattoo. It was obvious they weren't the man I was looking for. I paddled past them, rode a small wave into the beach and pulled my canoe up onto the sand. After I scanned the area for anyone with a yellow surfboard, I sat on the rock wall fronting Banyans and waited to see if Larry Johnson would show. I admired the pinkish purple hue on the surface of the ocean as the sun reflected off the low-hanging cotton candy colored clouds above.

It wasn't long before I spotted a yellow surfboard with a red lightning bolt headed my way. I checked for the tattoos Kathy had described. It was definitely Larry the dirtbag. She neglected to mention how big he was, oak tree kind of big. I paid him no attention so as not to tip him off until he passed by.

The last thing I wanted was to get into a brawl with a former MMA fighter. I made a mental note to recommend Kathy only date librarians in the future.

I put my canoe back into the water and slowly paddled out between the sets of waves behind Larry.

After paddling out, he sat atop of his board while he waited for the next set to roll in. I paddled up within ten feet, close enough to talk to him, but not close enough for him to attack me, since he wouldn't like what I would have to say.

I said, "Hey bra, so you like to hit women, yeah?"

He barked, "Who da fuck are you?"

His brow furrowed, fists clenched. It was clear he didn't like what he'd just heard and was ready to put a beating on me if I got any closer.

"Me? Payback Jack. It's your lucky day. I was going to kill you, but thought that was too good for you. Plus, it's too much risk for such little short-term reward. Instead, I decided to send you back to prison, so I wouldn't have to go myself for killing your sorry ass. Who knows, maybe I'll get lucky and someone in there will take you out after you've been there a while. See those cops and your parole officer?" I pointed with my paddle toward the beach.

"They're waiting for you. You can thank me for having your parole officer violate you. Walmart parking lot video, you got to love it. It clearly showed you slugging, Kathy. Then I watched you walk back to your car and jotted down your license plate."

Larry sneered at me and said, "When I get out, I'm coming for you, bra."

I smiled. "I've been threatened by the best. You'll have to get in line. You see the fire department rescue boat headed this way?"

Larry glanced north toward Kailua Bay.

I continued, "It's got cops onboard that are going to make sure you paddle in. You might as well catch a wave and enjoy the ride. It'll be the last one you take for quite some time."

Now that I had Larry headed off to jail, I turned the canoe and paddled slowly toward Kailua Bay. I could hear him cuss me as the rescue boat chased him toward the shore.

I savored in the satisfaction that I needn't worry anymore about that dirtbag hurting Kathy.

It turned out to be a beautiful morning as I watched the bustling activity in the bay, and thought all was well in the world, or at least Kailua town for the time being.

My phone rang, and I pulled it out of the dry bag inside the canoe and saw it was Grady.

When I answered, he said, "Where are you?"

"The middle of the bay in my canoe. Why, what's up?"

"Can you meet me at the pier in ten minutes?"

"Sure, I'll beach my canoe at the King Kam hotel."

Ten minutes later, I paddled into the small bay in front of the hotel. Grady was already there. I'd spent my career reading people, and the look on his face told me something was up, and I probably wouldn't like it.

CHAPTER TWELVE

Tourists were crowded onto the small beach in front of the King Kam hotel. I pulled my canoe from the lagoon and carried it off to the side of the beach. For privacy, Grady and I walked over to the pier that flanked the beach. We stood across from where the tour boats docked. Grady pulled a pack of cigarettes out of his shirt pocket and offered me one.

"No, thanks. Just stand up wind. I'll inhale as much as I can as the smoke drifts by."

"You're quitting again? How long has it been this time?"

"Six months, two weeks and a few hours, but who's counting?" I said as I glanced at my watch.

Grady nodded, lit a cigarette and took a drag. As he exhaled the smoke, he said, "Cook made bail this morning. That's the one drawback about arresting rich people. They almost always get out on bail."

I got a cheap hit of nicotine as I stood downwind. I savored the secondhand smoke as I breathed in deeply and replied, "No surprise, that new judge they got up at the courthouse is a real piece of work. He used to be a defense attorney."

Grady nodded, "I heard." He threw down the cigarette, firmly pivoted the heel of his shoe back and forth on it and said, "Fucking lawyers. There's got to be a better way."

"There is a better way. It's just illegal is the problem."

Grady grinned, "I wouldn't mind a vigilante taking care of Cook if, for some reason, he doesn't get convicted for trying to kill you. But I don't see that happening, since the video pretty much seals the deal."

"I thought about capping that piece of shit when I had him face down in the sand. But I also thought about going to prison, so here we are."

"If your aim would've been a little better when you put a bullet in him, that would've solved the problem."

I nodded. "I didn't wing him on purpose. I aimed for his heart. Guess I need more time at the range."

Grady lit another cigarette and blew smoke in my direction. He said, "Obviously."

I looked at my watch, "Thanks for the heads-up; I have to go get packed, I'm heading to Vegas tonight."

Grady reached into his back pocket and pulled out his wallet. He dug around inside it for a moment. "Found it," he said as he pulled out a tightly folded twenty dollar bill and handed it to me. "Put it in the first progressive slot machine you find, and we'll split the winnings."

"Not sure if or when I'll get a chance, but I'll try. It's a work trip. I'm doing a personal security gig for one of the tech billionaires that lives here part time. One of her regular security guys is out with the flu, so I was asked if I could fill in."

"I could use a part-time gig like that if you hear of any

openings in the future. I have about a year left before I retire," Grady said.

I nodded. "I'll keep it in mind." I took a couple of steps toward the beach to get my canoe and stopped. I turned back toward Grady. "I almost forgot to tell you, Sam Stuart put up a hundred grand to increase the reward money. Your phone should start blowing up pretty soon."

When I got back to the *Holo-Holo* Kathy was onboard, hard at work on her book. Pierre had tucked himself in right next to her on the couch. Lately, she'd spent more time on the boat than at her house. I don't doubt tongues wagged all over town that I'd taken up with a younger woman. But it wasn't that way at all. Occasionally, she'd hinted she might like me as a sugar daddy, but contrary to popular belief, there wasn't much sugar in it for her. Though I lived on a million dollar boat, I hadn't paid that for it. I may have looked rich, but I wasn't.

As far as paying my bills went, I wasn't hurting. My pension was enough to live on comfortably. My charters and part-time security work were the icing on the cake.

For Kathy, staying close to the boat was probably her way of owning a dog without actually having to take him home with her, which was just fine with me. I enjoyed having her around. She reminded me of my daughter.

I was starting to understand how her book was progressing just by the look on her face whenever I walked into the room. If her forehead was all scrunched up, it meant the story wasn't going well. A mild grin as she typed showed she was happy with the story. Today, she smiled and giggled periodically, so I assumed she was over the hump and in the home stretch. Every few minutes, she'd reach beside her and hand feed Pierre a treat. As far as I was concerned, he was definitely her dog now. It'd be a cold day in Kona before I'd feed him treats by hand.

When Kathy sat her computer down and got up to stretch, I said, "Good news, Larry's off to jail. And I'm going to Vegas tonight." I reached into my pocket and pulled out my wallet. "I'm going to be gone for a week, maybe longer. Here's five hundred bucks." I laid it on the table next to the galley. "If you need anything, just get it."

Kathy stared at me for a minute. "I don't see any bruises on you. And you're still alive. How'd you manage that?"

"It was easy kid, don't worry about it."

She let out a sigh and smiled as she went into the galley to make a pot of coffee. I sensed in her a genuine relief Larry would no longer be around.

"Can I go to Vegas with you?" Kathy yelled over the coffee grinder.

I shook my head and waited for her to stop grinding the coffee. "Sorry honey, it's a work trip. You and your boyfriend Pierre," I cut my eyes toward the couch, "need to hold down the fort until I get back."

CHAPTER THIRTEEN

It was eleven p.m. when I arrived at Air Services at the Kona airport. We were scheduled for departure at eleven-thirty. The other guys on the security team were already there. A ground crew member drove me out on the ramp to the Gulfstream jet to board. You got to love having your own plane. The billionaires live in another world that most of us never get a glimpse of, but I wouldn't trade places with them, even if it came with a jet. While being uber wealthy comes with a lot of perks, it also comes with a fair amount of danger.

Rich in obscurity would be my goal. Unfortunately for them, with bank accounts full of money, their anonymity went out the window right along with their safety and privacy. Now they have to pay people like me to shadow them for the rest of their lives. No thanks.

There wasn't a need to bring my weapon. There was a small armory onboard the plane, but I liked having my own tools, so I packed my Glock. Since I'm retired law enforcement, it was legal for me to carry a concealed weapon in all fifty states, which made me the first call when said billion-aire needed temporary armed security.

We landed at eight-thirty a.m. Nevada time and went straight to the boss's compound in Summerlin. She was scheduled for business meetings throughout the week. There weren't any recent threats against her, so I didn't expect any trouble. My part of the job was security for a couple of shopping trips between meetings, but otherwise I was free to do as I pleased until the return trip back to Hawaii.

The Big Island had gotten more crowded over the years since the arrival of the big box stores like Costco and Home Depot. Before they came to town, nobody was rushing to move to paradise. Back then, the only suppliers were mom-and-pop stores, and everything cost a fortune.

After the mass merchandisers put the small stores out of business, prices dropped considerably for common goods, and people flocked to the island in droves to live in paradise.

Me? I was pretty much over it and had been searching for a new place to live. Vegas had over a million people, which I wasn't crazy about living with. But outside of town looked like a viable possibility.

During my off time, I took a trip to Lake Las Vegas to check it out. You gotta love it, a man-made lake out in the middle of the desert. It had a couple of hotels and a nice golf course. The resort was only seventeen miles from the Las Vegas strip and away from the hustle and bustle of the city, but close enough when I wanted to go out on the town or see a show. I liked it so much I made an offer on a condo. Maybe I'd keep my boat in Kona and hire a captain to charter it out to cover the slip and maintenance overhead. Or I'd sell it. I was undecided and would have to consider the pros and cons.

All the way back to Kona, I thought about how I was going to break the news to Kathy that I'd bought a condo in Vegas. I was torn between two thoughts. Should I wait until she finished her book, or should I let her know right away, hoping that would motivate her to get her book done sooner rather than later? Those were the thoughts that occupied my brain until I looked out the window and saw snow-capped Mauna Kea in the distance. A snowy mountain in Hawaii always amazed me, no matter how many times I'd seen it before.

After the plane landed, the team and I escorted the client to her estate at Kukio, where the residence security took over and I was off duty.

On my way home to the harbor, I decided to keep the condo purchase to myself for the time being. I'd let Kathy finish her book, and then I'd spring it on her.

It was close to noon when I got back to the *Holo-Holo*. A shower and a nap were the first order of business. I hadn't gotten a full night's sleep the whole time I was in Vegas. I was surprised that Kathy wasn't there writing. Pierre was asleep on the fighting chair and briefly lifted his head to look my direction as I came onboard. There was a note slid under the door of the cabin. It said,

"I tried calling you, but your voicemail is full. I got bad news Jack, call me, Grady."

CHAPTER FOURTEEN

"What's up?" Jack asked when Grady answered his phone. "Kathy Medeiros was abducted early yesterday morning from the parking lot behind The Ugly Omelette. An old man, halfway across the lot, a regular at the restaurant, said he saw a man shove her into a van through an open side door as she walked by on her way to work. He couldn't provide much of a description. Apart from the assailant was Caucasian, wore all black, and had a ball cap pulled down over his eyes."

I listened patiently as Grady relayed the details. The pain in my gut grew more intense with every word he said. I wanted to avoid listening anymore, but had to.

Grady continued, "The kidnapper dumped Kathy at the end of Ali'i Drive. She was found by a woman out for a walk. The woman, a tourist, was a paramedic from Chicago, staying nearby in a condo next to the golf course. Beaten and stabbed multiple times, Kathy was barely alive. She would've bled to death if it wasn't for the Good Samaritan. The perp probably thought she was dead when he pushed her out of the van.

I have to warn you, she's in terrible shape because of the viciousness of the attack. I called her mother, but her number was disconnected. So, I dropped by her house, but she'd already moved off the island."

My heart sank the more Grady talked. I'd spent my career investigating violent crimes on military bases. It rarely bothered me because I didn't know the victim. This was different. First it was Miles, now Kathy. This was personal. The first thought that came to mind was revenge, then Aldrich Cook. "Aldrich Cook is who you need to look at," I said.

"I'm right there with you, Jack. I'm on my way to his office. I'll let you know how it plays out."

"Thanks. I'm going up to the hospital to see if they'll let me see Kathy."

"She's in Honolulu. They stabilized her at the Kona hospital and Life Flight took her to Queen's yesterday afternoon."

As I stared out the window of the Hawaiian Airlines jet on the way to Honolulu, I thought about who would've set out to kill Kathy. I knew her ex-boyfriend Larry was in jail, so it wasn't him.

Aldrich Cook was the only one I suspected. There weren't any secrets in a small town like Kona. Everyone knew Kathy was writing a book and using my boat as a place to work on it. Numerous people thought we were dating. We weren't. She was my hānai daughter, as far as I was concerned. I don't doubt Cook targeted her to get back at me.

The forty-minute flight felt like it took forever to get from Kona to Oahu. When I got to the hospital, I hoped

Kathy could tell me who had attacked her, but she'd slipped into a coma.

She was in intensive care, and Grady was right. I didn't recognize her when I entered her room. Her face was black and blue. Tubes and bandages covered most of her, from her waist up to the top of her head. Her prognosis for a full recovery wasn't good, according to her doctor.

I sat at Kathy's bedside for three days until her mother, Estelle, could fly to Honolulu from Las Vegas, where she'd moved.

"How is she?" Estelle whispered to me as she walked into the room for the first time. "You don't have to whisper. She's in a coma. Nothing's changed. She's still critical, but she's a fighter and hanging in there."

Estelle stood next to Kathy while she held her hand and nodded. She glanced at me with tear-swollen eyes. "She loves you like a father, Jack. You know that, right?"

I nodded. I wanted to avoid saying anything because I had to hold it together and not cry in front of Estelle. I was afraid if I said one word, the floodgates of my emotions would break loose and I wouldn't be able to stop them. I saved my tears for when I was alone in my hotel room.

To keep my composure, I bit into my bottom lip so hard I could taste the saltiness of blood. I reached into my shirt pocket and pulled out a hotel room key. I stood and handed it to Estelle. "This is to a room at the Ala Moana Hotel. It's about a mile and a half from here. You can stay there as long as you need to. After a few days here it will be good to get out, take a shower and recharge. I want to stay, but I need to go back to Kona and find the man who did this to Kathy."

"Do you know who's responsible?"

I shook my head. "But I'm going to find out." I looked at Kathy. "When she wakes up, ask her for a name."

Estelle nodded, and I walked out of the room, wondering if I'd ever see Kathy alive again. I said *when* she wakes up, but I really thought *if,* but didn't want to say it out loud.

On the flight back to Kona, the thought that ran through my mind over and over was that I was responsible because I told Kathy she didn't have to worry anymore. Larry was in jail, and it wouldn't be long before Cook was too. I should've seen this coming, was the thought in my head that overwhelmed all the others and played over and over like a broken record.

"Vengeance is mine," said the Lord, was another thought that I batted back and forth during the forty minute inter-island flight. But Jesus wasn't there, and I was, and Kathy deserved justice. Not being religious, I went with my plan instead, and who's to say the Lord wasn't working through me? Well, maybe the Glock wasn't his usual tool, but it was my weapon of choice.

By the time the plane landed, I'd decided that if Kathy died, I'd kill whoever was responsible. The thought of her killer living out their life in prison wasn't justice. I recalled when the Hawaii State Attorney General said on TV that if someone broke into your house to cause you harm, you should run out the back door. What a bunch of bullshit was the first thought that came to mind when I heard that. That's why society had become the way it was.

The criminals in Hawaii faced little, if any, consequences if they were arrested for anything less than murder. An eye for an eye was justice. Whoever had attacked Kathy should've prayed she didn't die.

When I got back to Kona, I picked up Pierre from the

kennel. It was the first time he'd ever been kind of happy to see me. When we got back onboard the *Holo-Holo* he went straight to his food bowl and ate until it was all gone. At the kennel, they said he ate about two bites of food and that was it. Poor little guy. After he ate, he shadowed me everywhere I went. "Don't worry buddy, it's going to be okay." I grabbed a new chew toy out of the galley and tossed it out the cabin door into the cockpit. He raced out of the cabin and pounced on it, then dragged it into the shade under the fighting chair and went to work on it.

While Pierre gnawed on his chew toy, I called Grady to see if he had any leads in Miles' case and what Cook had to say when Grady went to his office.

The first question I had for Grady was, "Where was Cook when Kathy was attacked?"

"He had an alibi that was corroborated by witnesses."

"Then he paid somebody to do it. Kathy has a history with Cook. If you talk to her boss, Jeff, he'll confirm that she wouldn't even wait on Cook anymore and that Jeff had to deal with him when he came into the restaurant. Plus, I wouldn't doubt he'd go after her to get back at me."

Grady said, "I hear you, my phone's beeping, I got to go. I'm expecting a call from the deputy DA handling Cook's case. He left a message earlier and said there was a problem with the evidence. I better take the call."

CHAPTER FIFTEEN

I couldn't sit on the boat and do nothing, so I grabbed a beer and Pierre's leash. We strolled out to the mouth of the harbor, sat on the rocks, and watched the boats come and go. Salt air and the sea had always been therapeutic for me. We sat for about a half hour while I attempted to quiet my mind and think about what the next step should be.

A few minutes after I took the last sip of beer, my stomach growled. It demanded either food or more alcohol. As much as I wanted to crawl inside a bottle and check out of reality, I resisted the thought and made the correct choice. Pierre and I headed over to the Harbor restaurant to grab something to eat, since it was nearby. It was the first time I'd had an appetite in over a week, so I thought I'd better eat while I felt like it. I had no desire to go to The Ugly Omelette because I didn't want to talk about what had happened to Kathy, and her co-workers would surely want an update on her condition. I wasn't ready to face that.

The Harbor restaurant was open air on three sides, with a bar at one end. As long as Pierre kept a low profile, nobody would say anything. I tucked him in under my arm, and he was barely noticeable as we headed to a table. I took a seat at a table in the corner that had a view of the marina, with my back to the wall.

The waitress was friendly; she wasn't very chatty, but that was ok, I wasn't either, and had no desire to be. I ordered and not long afterward she brought my fish sandwich and a hamburger patty for Pierre. He laid at my feet under the table, and I put his plate beside him.

I took a bite of my sandwich and stared off aimlessly toward the entrance when two guys walked in. I recognized one of them. They sat a couple of tables away, and I overheard them order a couple of beers. I noticed something right away about the one I didn't know. He sat facing toward me and wore a fishhook necklace. That wasn't unusual. What was is that it was made of abalone. The only one I'd ever seen like it belonged to Miles. It was a custom design hand carved by a local craftsman made from an abalone shell. I texted Grady when I saw it. He texted back he was on his way. His ETA was less than five minutes, since the police station was less than a mile away from the harbor.

The man with his back to me was a local charter captain named Rudy Gutierrez. I didn't know him well. We'd spoken in passing a couple of times at the annual billfish tournament. After I finished eating and Pierre had licked every morsel of hamburger from his plate, I stopped at their table on the way out the door and said, "Howzit?"

Rudy nodded, "Hey Jack. What's up?"

"I read in the paper your boat won the Wahine's tournament a few weeks ago."

He smiled. "Yeah, those women can fish."

I looked at his partner and said, "Nice hook. Where'd you get it?"

The man swallowed hard. Apparently I'd struck a nerve.

"A friend gave it to me," he finally said after he almost choked.

"Does this friend have a name?"

"You writing a book?" Rudy said with a hint of annoyance, while his friend remained silent. I glanced at Rudy, "That hook came from a friend of mine too—a dead friend. Now there's an ongoing murder investigation." I turned my focus back to the man wearing the hook. "Now–how did you get the hook?"

"Are you a cop?" he snapped.

"Nope–but my friend is."

"I don't see your friend."

I looked toward the front entrance with a sigh of relief as Grady made his way past the bar.

When no-name turned to look, he saw Grady and jumped up to run, but instead got a face full of teeth when Pierre attempted to leap from my arm and rip his face off. Mr. No-name looked like the victim in one of those alien movies where all you saw was the creature on the victim's face. I thought it was physically impossible to reverse motion that fast, but the man was back in the chair before Pierre got his fangs into him.

There wasn't any doubt in my mind the man had Miles' necklace because it had a little red speck on the very tip of the hook. There was no way there were two hooks carved from an abalone shell that were identical like that. Pierre seemed to confirm it by the way he had gone after the guy.

When Grady got to the table, it was clear he knew the man when he said, "Hey Louis, you can stand up now and put your hands behind your back."

While Grady cuffed him, he said, "Thanks Jack, I've

been looking for Louis Atkins for a while. He's got a warrant out for burglary."

At the station, Grady allowed me to watch him interview Louis in a small room via closed-circuit TV. Grady sat across the table from him, and after he read Louis his rights, Grady pointed at the hook. "Where'd you get that necklace?"

"A man traded it for some work I did."

"What's his name?"

"He's that realtor that advertises on TV all the time, Aldrich Cook."

CHAPTER SIXTEEN

Pierre sat nearby while I got dressed. He carefully watched as I adjusted my tie. He probably hoped I'd strangle myself with it. Our relationship had actually improved since I think he realized I seemed to be the one in charge of his eating dinner regularly. At least he'd quit growling at me for sport.

I dressed for court like I'd done a thousand times before. When I retired, I thought I was done going to court. Miles deserved justice, and I was going to see that he got it because justice mattered.

It was the first day of Aldrich Cook's trial, and I looked forward to seeing him go to prison. Cook had hired a top Honolulu lawyer to handle his case. She was a regular on the nightly cable news channels defending the dirtbag of the week. I'd seen her get people off that definitely should've been convicted. I was confident that wouldn't be the case this time since we had the video evidence of Cook attacking me.

Before I left the boat, I checked myself in the mirror and decided that was as good as it was going to get.

On my way out the door of the salon, I threw a handful of dog bones into the cockpit.

Pierre was one step behind me. "Sorry buddy, you have to stay here today. Here are a few extra bones to tide you over until I get back." I tossed them into the shade under the fighting chair as I stepped off the back of the *Holo-Holo* onto the dock. He grabbed the nearest bone and got to work. He didn't even look my way as I left the boat. At least he'd quit giving me stink eye.

Before court, I was on my way to meet Grady for coffee. We agreed to try a new ocean front coffee place on Ali'i Drive near the old Bubba Gump's.

The place was busy, and I grabbed a corner table on the outdoor patio while I waited for Grady to arrive. The table was less than ten feet from the edge of Kailua Bay. I watched as a school of yellow tangs nibbled algae off the rocks in the shallows. They swayed back and forth with the tide like the pendulum of a clock. The water in the middle of the bay was turquoise, and it looked like the perfect day to go for a swim. As much as I'd like to have gotten into the ocean after court, first I had to call Estelle for an update on Kathy.

My mind wandered about what the future would bring while I waited. Moving off the island, Miles, Kathy, it was almost all too much to think about at one time, and Grady was late. It was unusual for him to be late. Another five minutes passed before he finally walked through the doorway to the patio.

"Sorry I'm late, Jack. I was on the phone with the deputy DA handling Cook's case. There's a problem with the evidence."

"Problem? The video of Cook attacking me is pretty compelling, don't you think?

"That's not the problem. The video has gone missing from the evidence room at the station."

I pounded on the table. "You're fucking kidding me, right?" The early morning chatter of diners having breakfast fell silent as I had clearly interrupted them. People turned their attention toward our table to see what the commotion was about. I didn't look at them, and neither did Grady. When it was clear, there wasn't any more to see. The morning chatter continued as if nothing had happened. I'd always been good at stuffing my emotions over the years, but the video that just disappeared was too much to bear.

Grady shook his head. "I wish I were kidding. There's no way to prove who took it, just like the fifty grand that disappeared out of there years ago. The DA said, Find the video, and he'll refile the case."

I stood up and screamed, "Fuck!" loud enough to be heard on the other side of the island. I threw a tip down on the table and said, "I'll be in touch. I have to go." Grady nodded and took a sip of coffee like nothing happened.

While I drove back to the harbor, I thought about the chances of recovering the video. But first I needed to find out if Aldrich Cook was responsible for Kathy's attack too, and if he was, he definitely had to die.

CHAPTER SEVENTEEN

On my way back to the boat, I stopped at the post office to pick up my mail. The last thing I wanted to see when I pulled my mail out of the PO Box was a notification to pick up a certified letter. I had not one, but two notifications.

My gut told me they weren't good news. Nothing good had ever come in a certified letter addressed to me. I took the notification slips to the pickup counter, and the clerk handed me two certified letters. I didn't have a clue as to what they were about.

Both letters were from law firms, one I recognized, the other I didn't. I could see it had become a let's go home and get drunk kind of day.

My next stop was the liquor store at the harbor. I picked up a fresh bottle of tequila to numb the impending doom the letters most likely contained. Between the letters and the stolen video, it definitely looked like the trifecta of a rotten day. I'd had just about all I could stand, and it wasn't even noon yet.

When I got back to the *Holo-Holo*, Pierre was lying in the shade under the fighting chair. I had to dodge little piles of puke where he'd upchucked his dog bones. He did his best to eat them all in one sitting. The evidence was clear he wasn't a self-feeder, and I knew little about dogs.

After I'd cleaned up the mess, I went into the salon and sat the bottle of tequila and letters on the table next to the galley. I grabbed a letter opener and a shot glass, then took a seat.

If I'd taken a couple of shots first, there was an excellent chance I wouldn't have read the letters. So I compromised and took a shot, then opened each letter.

It had been weeks since the last time I had a drink. I didn't particularly care for the taste of alcohol; it was the warmth in my belly and the eight seconds of ecstasy when it hit my brain that kept me coming back for more.

I opened the letter from the law firm I recognized first. It was from an ambulance chaser in Honolulu. Aldrich Cook was demanding payment for his medical costs related to the bullet I'd put in his shoulder. He also wanted fifty thousand dollars for pain and suffering. *Yeah, people in hell want ice water. The balls on that guy* was the first thought that came to mind. I took another shot of tequila as I regretted missing his heart. I was really beginning to regret not capping him when I had him face down in the sand the night he attacked me.

I promised myself I'd get back to a monthly trip to the gun range after I moved to Las Vegas. In my defense, the only range on the island was in Hilo, a hundred miles away on the other side of the island.

Since I'd retired, I hadn't wanted to make the two hundred mile round trip since I didn't need to re-qualify for the job anymore. In hindsight, if I had, Cook would've been nothing but a bad memory.

I took another shot of fire water to suppress the guilt

over Kathy and opened the second letter. It was from an attorney named Ed Miller.

I read the letter and felt relieved he wasn't suing me. Quite the contrary, it was the first positive thing that had happened that day. The letter said Mr. Miller was handling Miles Goodmunson's estate. It also said Miles had left everything to Pierre, and that I would be the trustee of the money.

It just confirmed, to me, I didn't know Miles as well as I thought I had. I would never have dreamt he had an estate, much less him having left it to Pierre.

I called Miller's office and his secretary said I could come to the office later that afternoon. As curious as I was, I knew I would be in no condition, and said I'd call back and make an appointment when I had a better idea of my schedule.

My mission at that moment was to crawl into the tequila bottle for the rest of the day. But first, I had to call Estelle and get an update on Kathy's condition before I got too drunk.

CHAPTER EIGHTEEN

I took a sip of tequila and dialed Estelle's phone number.

It rang so long I began to count the rings. She finally answered on the umpteenth ring with a barely audible, "Hello."

Estelle's voice cracked as she said, "Kathy's had a stroke. She has swelling on the brain."

My gut tightened. "What's the prognosis?"

"The doctor says she's not responding to the medication, and her chances aren't good. He said there's a new experimental drug he's having flown in that is her only hope."

There was a long silence on the line when Estelle broke it with, "If you believe in God, Jack, now's the time to pray."

Tears pooled in my eyes, and as they flowed down my cheeks, they dripped into my shot glass. Tears and tequila; not my drink of choice.

"I'm on my way, Estelle," I said as I abruptly hung up.

I considered taking another shot before I left, but opted to put the tequila bottle in the liquor cabinet instead.

I was still sober enough to fly to Oahu and packed an

overnight bag. Pierre sensed something was up as he watched me brush my teeth and gargle to hide the smell of alcohol.

The first stop on the way to the airport was the kennel. Pierre growled at me as we approached the front door. "Shut up. I'm not in the mood for it today." He could tell from my tone I was serious and did just that.

During the forty-five minute flight to Oahu, I thought about my daughter Elizabeth and the similarities between her and Kathy. When Elizabeth died, a piece of me died with her that day.

Many years had passed since that time, and my friendship with Kathy had done a lot to fill the void. Now it looked like I faced losing another sweet girl in my life, and I wasn't ready for it.

I was certain if anyone talked to me on the plane, I'd probably cry. To prevent that, I focused on the anger that stirred in my gut. I thought about how unfair the whole thing was in each situation. Elizabeth's death was a freak accident. While Kathy hadn't died yet, it appeared likely from what Estelle said the doctor had told her.

Both Elizabeth and Kathy had suffered consequences that weren't fair and paid a price. Until the perpetrator who'd hurt Kathy had justice served upon him, I vowed to myself to not shed one more tear.

Kathy was a year younger than Elizabeth, and I had allowed her a place near my heart that I never thought I would've allowed anyone ever again.

The flight attendant's announcement we were descending into Honolulu jolted me out of the circular thought I'd been going round and round with since we left Kona.

I looked out the window and saw Diamond Head off to

the right. It brought back fond memories of Elizabeth and I racing to the top of the extinct volcano when she was a teenager. I smiled as I thought about how she'd beat me, and teased me all the way home about how I was over the hill.

It was the last happy memory we had together before she'd fallen off her horse the next day. It was a freak accident. She hit her head on the only rock within a hundred yards and died that night from a cerebral hemorrhage. A cat scan would've probably saved her life. She hadn't told me or her mother about the fall until it was too late.

The ride from the airport to Queen's hospital didn't take long. Traffic was light, which was unusual for Honolulu. Angie, my ex-wife, was a nurse there, and I hoped to not run into her.

We'd had a good marriage until Elizabeth died. Angie never outright blamed me, but I'm sure she felt I was responsible, since I was the one who'd bought the horse as a surprise birthday gift.

I'd managed to avoid Angie the last time I was there. The chances of running into her were slim since she was an ER nurse and Kathy was in the ICU.

Estelle met me outside the door to Kathy's room and said, "The hospital is only allowing one visitor at a time. I've already seen her. You can go in now."

When I opened the door, there stood Angie next to Kathy's bed, attending to the bandage on her head. So much for avoiding Angie. It was now officially the second-worst day of my life. The last time I saw her was when we signed divorce papers. The dissolution of our marriage was amicable, so I didn't expect any trouble, but I wanted to avoid feeling like I was reliving the death of Elizabeth either. By the time I got to Honolulu, the day had gotten worse by the hour.

Angie's brow narrowed. She said, "Jack, you know her?"

I nodded. "She's a close friend. How is she?" Angie shook her head. "It's not good. But she's got another good doctor treating her now. He's new here and a former army doctor that has a lot of head trauma experience from working in Afghanistan."

My back was to the door when I heard the click of the door handle. "You're about to meet him. His name is Dr. Shelly," Angie said.

He was a big man, mid to late forties, with enough grey hair that I sensed he'd been around the block a time or two. Estelle followed behind and stood next to me. Angie was always a stickler for rules, but ignored the only one visitor at a time rule.

Dr. Shelly went straight to Kathy and barely acknowledged my presence, which I was fine with. Heal her and we'll talk later. As much as I wanted to play twenty questions, I stood back and kept quiet as I watched him examine Kathy. His face showed no emotion as he injected her with the experimental drug that had just arrived from the airport.

Dr. Shelly looked up at me and asked, "Are you her father?" I shook my head. "Not biologically, but I care for her like my own." Estelle interjected, "Anything you tell me, you can tell Jack." Dr. Shelly nodded, "Now we wait."

Angie and Dr. Shelly left the room, and Estelle and I stood on each side of Kathy. I put my hand over Kathy's. Estelle did the same and then reached over the bed to grab my hand. She lightly squeezed and said, "Thy will be done."

CHAPTER NINETEEN

Estelle and I sat with Kathy all night. When morning came, I stood and stretched as I felt the warmth of the sun's rays shine through the window into the room.

When Estelle went to get us coffee, I stood in front of the window and bathed in the sunlight while I wondered if the experimental medicine had made a difference.

I got my answer when I turned and saw Kathy's eyes try to open. The more they opened, the more my own pooled with tears of gratitude. I reached for her hand and lightly held it close to my face.

The investigator in me wanted to ask her if Cook had attacked her, but the father in me said now wasn't the time. The last thing I wanted to do was cause her any more trauma.

A moment later, Estelle returned with coffee. She almost dropped both cups when she saw Kathy awake.

I pushed the button on the wall to call for a nurse as Angie walked in the door right after Estelle. She smiled when she saw Kathy was awake and said, "I told you Dr. Shelly was good."

My gut tightened each time Kathy drifted in and out of consciousness. Angie read my face the first time it happened, and said, "It's normal. She'll stay awake longer and longer as time goes on."

After the morning excitement of Kathy coming out of the coma, Angie ushered Estelle and me out of the room so Dr. Shelly could run tests without us in the way.

Later that morning, after he had examined Kathy, he came and found Estelle and me in the waiting room. He said, "She'll have a long road to recovery, and only time will tell how much damage the stroke has caused."

After Dr. Shelly left, Estelle cried. "I don't know what I'm going to do. I live in a crappy motel room. I can't take care of her there."

"You don't have to stay there. I have a three-bedroom condo at Lake Las Vegas. You and Kathy can stay there while she rehabs. I insist."

"You've done so much, Jack. How can I ever repay you? I'm broke as a church mouse. The sale of my house got me out from under a mortgage I couldn't afford, but there was only enough money left over to move to Vegas."

"No worries Estelle. I wasn't kidding when I said I cared for Kathy as one of my own. It'll all work out. It always does."

Estelle cried again, "I don't even have airfare for her."

"Like I said, no worries. I have enough airline miles. You both can fly to Vegas."

Estelle nodded as she wiped the tears away with a handkerchief she had pulled from her purse.

I smiled, "Done. I have to go back to Kona to take care of some business. Before I leave, I'm going to say goodbye to Kathy. Later, I'll call you for an update."

Kathy was awake when I entered her room and Angie

was changing the bandage on her head and said, "Keep it brief. She needs her rest."

I nodded. The investigator side of me couldn't resist any longer. "Do you know who attacked you?"

"I don't remember anything. All I know is my head hurts."

"Okay, honey, you get some rest. I have to go back to Kona to find who did this to you." She nodded off again, and I kissed her on the cheek goodbye, and left for the airport.

On the plane back to Kona, I planned how I would deal with Cook if it turned out he was responsible. The way I saw it, if he wasn't in prison, the only way Kathy would ever be safe would be for him to die. If the video of him attacking me were to surface, that would solve the problem, but the chances of that happening were about zero.

I'd be the last thing Cook ever saw on this planet if he didn't go to prison. I had it all figured out. I'd abduct him and make him walk the plank twenty miles off the west side of the Big Island.

As far as I was concerned, making him walk the plank gave him a chance. That was, if he could overcome the current that flowed toward Japan. If he could swim back to the island, he would live, if not, adios asshole.

Hell, superman would be halfway to Japan before he'd be able to get out of that invisible river headed to the Far East. I thought about many scenarios for killing Cook that were more painful and messy, but setting the stage for Mother Nature to take care of him was the remedy I kept coming back to the more I thought about it.

CHAPTER TWENTY

I picked up Pierre on my way back to the *Holo-Holo*. His tail was a blur when he saw it was me who'd come to break him out of jail. For the first time, he acted as if he was genuinely glad to see me.

Up to that point, I hadn't really considered him a real dog or man's best friend. The first thought that came to mind whenever I thought about him was a small furry alligator with a bad attitude.

It surprised me I was happy to see him too, since he was definitely an acquired taste. It probably had something to do with him not trying to bite me at first sight.

When I got back to the boat, I took Pierre for a walk out to the mouth of the harbor. We both needed the exercise, and I needed some salt air in my lungs. We sat on a big rock and watched a pod of dolphins swim by in between the fishing boats that came and went.

It reminded me about the time I fostered Kiki and Koa for the Navy. They were like the dogs of the sea, but with millions of dollars spent on training them to be warriors. Of course, the Navy wasn't happy when they found out I'd added to their dolphin's skill set. I'd trained them to help me catch fish on my charters. I still miss them. They were the best fisherman I'd ever worked with.

The eventual move to Vegas would be the right thing for me, but I'd miss the ocean. First, I had business to take care of. Miles and Kathy both deserved justice. I'd see to it they got it before I left the island.

I called Grady to see if he'd gotten any tips from the reward line. "Hey Jack, while you were at the hospital, Louis Atkins made a deal with the DA to shave some time off his sentence by giving up the thug who attacked Kathy."

"No shit?"

"I told him he looked at being charged as an accessory to murder since he had Miles' necklace, and he was facing some serious jail time. It was enough to scare him into making a deal. It gets even better. We picked up the guy who attacked Kathy, and he's going to roll over on Cook."

"What's this shit-bird's name?"

"Ricky Silva. He's a real piece of work with a rap sheet going back to when he was in a sperm cell. I'm pretty sure there was a warrant out for him the day he was born."

"They need a three strikes law here, instead of the current catch and release program."

"You're singing to the choir, Jack."

I breathed a sigh of relief as I listened to Grady. This time, Cook would go to prison for a long time and I wouldn't have to risk prison myself for killing him.

"Outstanding work, Grady. Dinner is on me. We'll have to go out to the Marlin House and celebrate when this is all over."

"Deal, and we can celebrate my retirement, too."

"You're finally going to pack it in, huh? I thought your plan was to wait another year?"

"I was, but after word gets around that I'm looking for the rat that stole your video out of the evidence locker, I'll be on the wrong side of the blue wall. Don't get me wrong, there's some good people I work with, but there are also a couple of rat bastards here that are crooked as a dog's hind leg. I have a pretty good idea which one of those fuckers stole the video. Now it's just a matter of connecting the dots."

"I don't envy the animosity that's going to generate for you, but I appreciate the dedication to doing what's right. As payback, I'll hook you up with my billionaire out at Kukio. She will have an opening when I move to Vegas. She's always traveling and needs security. You'll make more working for her part-time than you do now working full time."

"Vegas–You know it's hotter than a Mexican jail cell there, right?"

I laughed. I always appreciated the way Grady said what he thought.

"You might be right, but I need a change of scenery. After all this is over, I'm retiring for good. My plan is to sit in an air-conditioned casino, drink beer, play video poker, and flirt with the cocktail waitresses."

Grady laughed. He said, "You'll be back. Everyone always comes back, and then we'll start a private investigation firm."

"Don't hold your breath."

During the conversation with Grady, I sat on the couch and eventually noticed the certified letters on the end table next to the couch. They reminded me I needed to go see the lawyer about Miles' estate. Pierre sat on the deck facing toward me, his ears perked up as he stared. It was as if he knew it was time to get stuff done.

"I have to go see a lawyer."

"What's his name?"

"Ed Miller."

Grady paused for a moment. "He's a probate lawyer, right?"

"That's correct, he's handling Miles' estate."

Grady laughed again. "Miles and estate aren't the two words I'd expect to hear in the same sentence. I don't understand the world we live in anymore."

"Me either. I'll explain more later after I see the lawyer."

After I got off the phone, I looked down at Pierre. He was still on my lap. I continued to scratch behind his ears for a minute before I said, "Okay buddy, time to go."

CHAPTER TWENTY-ONE

Ed Miller's office was on the second floor of the ocean front Kona Inn in the village. His wife Shirley ran the office. She had been after me to get down there for over a week.

When I opened the door to the small office, Shirley smiled and said, "Hi Pierre." She looked at me and said, "You must be Jack."

I nodded. "Have a seat, and Ed will be with you shortly." I smiled and parked myself in an old leather chair that was probably put there in the 1920s when the Kona Inn was first built.

Before I had time to open a magazine, Ed stuck his head out from behind his office door and said, "Hi Pierre," and, like Shirley, then glanced at me. He said, "Come on back," as he held the door open.

I asked, "Everyone here knows Pierre. How is that?"

Mr. Miller smiled. "Technically, we all work for him now. You're the vehicle of how he gets here. Miles always brought him when he came to the office, so we'd know who the boss was when and if the day came when Miles was gone."

Miller could see the narrowing of my brow would require further explanation.

"Miles set up a trust to take care of Pierre in the event of his death."

My brow still hadn't relaxed as I listened.

"In a nutshell, he continued, Miles left property for a dog park and a homeless shelter. He also left money for Pierre. Miles was the sole heir to a well-known candy company. You'll get a hundred thousand per year as payment to take care of Pierre. His trust fund will cover any expenses necessary for his well-being. Though Miles didn't care to live indoors, he stated in his will that you could use whatever funds needed to house Pierre if need be."

I sighed as I glanced down at Pierre for a moment. I looked back up at Miller, "You're telling me Pierre is rich like the dog in New York that Leona Helmsley left millions of dollars to?"

Miller smiled. "That's right, I believe she left her dog something like twelve million. Pierre is richer."

The crease in my brow was back, because if word got out Miles had left a fortune to his dog, it would be an enormous pain in my ass security wise. Pierre would become like the billionaire who couldn't leave home without protection.

I laughed and said, "Miles was smart by him leaving Pierre to me. He knew the dog would have armed security for the rest of his life."

Miller smiled but said nothing.

I asked, "Who knows about this?"

"Just you, me, and my wife, Shirley."

After I signed some papers, I and the newfound golden goose left Miller's office and headed back to the harbor after running a few errands while in town.

When I got back to the *Holo-Holo* the first order of business was to have a drink and think about what had just transpired at Ed Miller's office. Learning Miles was a trust fund baby blew my mind. He'd never let on he came from a wealthy family, or that he had any family to speak of. He'd lived the life of a beach bum. Who would've thought?

I poured a gin and tonic and sat on the couch while I looked through a pile of mail I'd picked up on my way home. Most of it was junk mail and bills. There was another letter from the ambulance chaser representing Cook. It sat on top of the pile. The more I looked at it, the higher my blood pressure rose. I called his scumbag lawyer to tell him what he and his client could do. It probably wasn't the smartest thing to do, but I did it anyway.

I was really missing the stolen video of Cook attacking me, since that would have quashed the whole thing.

"Tell your client to go fuck himself," was the extent of the conversation I had with the ambulance chaser. "We'll see you in court," was his parting shot.

I wasn't worried. They had no case. It was a shakedown attempt, and the definition of a frivolous lawsuit. It was Cook's word against mine. Initially, his reputation was all but destroyed after his arrest and the subsequent negative publicity. But soon after his arrest, he'd made a couple of large donations to local charities, trying to rehabilitate his image. And once again, he said he would donate money for a homeless shelter. So far, it had been just talk. However, it worked based on half the letters to the editor I'd read in the last Sunday paper.

Cook told anyone who'd listen he was being framed and continued to tell the same lie over and over since his arrest, and people had fallen for it. They didn't want to believe a fine upstanding citizen like Cook could be a murderer, much less the West Side Slasher, as the newspaper had rightly insinuated in its reporting. The real test would be what a jury thought when he went to trial for paying Ricky Silva to kill Kathy.

CHAPTER TWENTY-TWO

I took one of the last seats in the back of the small gallery at the old Kona courthouse. It was a good thing I got there early because seats had filled up unusually fast. All the major media outlets from Honolulu had reporters there to cover the trial. It had become standing room only in the back because of them and the gadflies who had nothing else better to do than watch the trial, then write letters to the editor afterward about how the trial should've really gone. A couple of those old guys no doubt would've been better judges than some of the ones appointed to the bench.

Aldrich Cook had hired top Honolulu criminal defense lawyer Tyler Blake. He had a reputation for trying his cases in the media and excelled at it. For weeks, he'd told any reporter who'd listen that Cook was the victim. Blake called the trial *The Great Injustice.* He'd done all the morning and evening news shows and even got on a couple of mainland cable networks to promote his version of the facts. They were pure fiction, but that didn't seem to matter to him. The guy was good, really good. I had a sour feeling in my gut when I thought about the potential outcome of the trial.

That was due to the fact that if he told the same lie long enough, people would begin to believe it. The jury pool wasn't that big in Kona, and no doubt a lot of them would believe what Blake was selling as the truth.

While Ricky Silva was the star witness who'd testify Cook paid him to attack Kathy, a conviction was a long way from being a done deal.

The packed courtroom was a testament to Blake's ability to get reporters salivating like hungry dogs for a story.

When Blake and Cook arrived, it was a spectacle outside the courthouse. I would've sworn he'd paid protesters to hold a rally out front. That wasn't typical for Kona, even in a high-profile case. A couple of murders the previous year had never drawn that kind of attention. I would've expected something like that in Honolulu, but never Kona.

The circus looked like the time when Michael Jackson was facing charges, and danced on the roof of his SUV outside the courthouse in California after he'd plead not guilty.

Tyler Blake was mid-forties, tanned, with close-cropped jet black hair. He wore an Armani suit, Rolex watch, and Italian leather shoes. He looked like a model for a Fortune 500 company magazine. I envisioned, during the trial, all the female jurors swooning over him and taking whatever nonsense he said as gospel.

He looked the part compared to Deputy District Attorney Henry Stanford, who still had pimples, a cheap suit, and was fresh out of law school. Not only that, but Stanford looked so young, he could've been mistaken for Doogie Howser.

· · ·

Everyone stood when the bailiff bellowed, "All rise," as Judge Sherman Clark entered the room. That sour feeling in my gut earlier had returned full force. I wasn't expecting him. Clark was as liberal as they came and wasn't supposed to be the judge handling the trial. Before his appointment to the bench, he was a local defense attorney. More than once I'd read in the paper a decision of his that made me shake my head in disbelief. It seemed Kona had become a haven for career criminals who'd face little consequence for their crimes when they appeared before Clark. He got the case at the last minute when the original judge assigned had a conflict and had to recuse himself.

The case was now officially a coin toss in my mind. It would all come down to jury selection. I recognized Richard Smart, seated at the defense table. He was one of the most high-profile jury consultants in the industry. I was familiar with him because the Honolulu US District Attorney had used him on a case I was involved in before I retired.

The County of Hawaii barely had the money to pay Stanford, much less hire a consultant. My gut was officially wrecked from the uncertainty. The thought of Cook getting off made me angry. I thought about how I would make him walk the plank about twenty miles off the coast if he were acquitted. I'd always believed in the rule of law, but if the jury found Cook not guilty, I swore to myself he'd pay for what he had done to Miles and Kathy—no matter what. Besides, I'm old enough now, a life sentence doesn't scare me like it used to.

The first potential juror was a man named Joe Watkins. He looked as if he was in his fifties and was an auto mechanic. Blake asked him, "Have you formed any opinions about the case?"

Mr. Watkins smiled and paused for a moment before he

answered. He looked straight at Cook and said, "I have no doubt he's guilty. I eat at the Ugly Omelette regularly, and I've seen the way he harassed Kathy Medeiros while she worked. Everyone knows he's the West Side Slasher, too. His phony persona of being a great philanthropist is just a marketing ploy to fool the public. He should be hung right outside the courthouse. The world would be better off without the likes of him." I caught myself nodding in agreement. He was a man after my own heart. The world needed more men like him. Too bad. He was quickly excused from the jury. As much as I agreed with his opinion of Cook. I wished he would've kept that to himself and stayed on the jury.

By the end of the day, the jury had been picked. Six women and six men from various walks of life. It felt more and more like a coin toss.

I had to give Doogie Howser props after the first day. He tried to get the judge to issue a gag order, but was unsuccessful. If I were to compare it to a baseball game, I'd say the prosecution was down one run right from the start. The next day would be opening statements. Just how good Doogie would be, since he was the unknown factor, left an uneasy feeling in my gut.

Blake was a gunslinger. Cook hired the best lawyer money could buy in Hawaii, and probably almost any other place. Tomorrow would be the test.

CHAPTER TWENTY-THREE

Blake had finished his opening statement just in time for lunch. I met Grady down the street from the courthouse at a new hamburger joint in a strip mall. I'd heard the food was good. The other thing I heard more than once was Cook would be acquitted. That was if you were to believe the letters to the editor in the local paper. Half the town thought he was a saint, and the other half the devil incarnate. Hopefully, the jury was from the latter. The burger joint was one of those little hole-in-the-wall places where you ordered at the counter inside. While Grady and I waited for our food, he asked me about my impression of Stanford and if I thought he had a chance against Blake.

I shook my head. "I've watched the women in the jury as Blake made his opening statement. I fully expect a couple of them to throw their panties at him before this trial's over. We are so screwed."

Grady nodded. "When I worked in Honolulu, I had cases where the perps were guilty as shit and they were solid cases. But they walked free because they had Blake as their lawyer. That guy could sell ice to an Eskimo on the jury."

I sighed while my stomach gurgled. I couldn't tell if it was from the case or I was just hungry. "Any tips come in lately?" I asked, as our food arrived at the table.

Grady shook his head as he took a bite of his burger. I'd really hoped the increase in the reward would've led to a witness who could put Cook at the scene of Miles' or any of the other murders. I hated the fact that everything rode on Cook's trial. A conviction would give us time to gather evidence in the other murders. Hopefully, to lock him up for the rest of his life. But so far, it didn't look good. It would all come down to Ricky Silva testifying after lunch.

When I got back to the courthouse parking lot, the only things missing were the carnival rides. The three-ring circus, fueled by the media, was in full effect. I got back just in time to get the last seat in the back of the courtroom.

Judge Clark asked Mr. Stanford, "Are you ready to proceed?"

Stanford shook his head and said, "Your honor, we can't locate our witness and request a continuance until tomorrow morning."

Judge Clark looked toward the defense table and said, "Do you have any problem with that, Mr. Blake?" He shook his head and replied, "No, your honor." Cook had a smug look on his face, as if he knew the key witness would be a no show. That sour feeling in my gut that had come and gone was now a permanent fixture.

I was on my way back to the *Holo-Holo* when Grady texted me. "*Ricky Silva was found dead. It looks like a professional hit. He's got two large caliber bullet holes in the head and one in the chest."*

The case against Cook was over. I knew it, everyone involved knew it. The next morning, Stanford withdrew the case against Cook.

That night, Grady stopped by the *Holo-Holo* to have a beer and talk story about what had happened.

"The hitter was waiting for Silva. When he got in his car, the guy walked up and shot him through the driver's side window. None of the neighbors heard or saw anything."

I shook my head. "We have to find the stolen video. It's the only way Cook is ever going to see the inside of a jail cell. I'm going to put out a reward for it. Even if I have to sell my boat to raise the money."

Grady grimaced. "Don't sell your boat just yet. I've narrowed it down to two guys who had access to the evidence locker at the time the video went missing. Let me lean on them first." I nodded and handed Grady another beer.

After we finished our beers and Grady left, I started thinking about the best place to make Cook walk the plank.

CHAPTER TWENTY-FOUR

The next morning, before I headed to Oahu, I went to get Pierre and my go bag. He was still asleep on the couch, where he knew he wasn't supposed to be. I made sure all of his toys were in the bag, and we had enough snacks for the trip.

He growled at me as I went to pick him up. He probably thought we were going to the kennel again, since lately he'd become a regular inmate there. When he showed me his fangs, it was clear he'd had enough of being a jailbird. Up to that point, I'd viewed his ill will toward me as unjustified. But I didn't blame him one bit, since his life had been turned upside down since Miles' murder.

In the most excited voice I could muster that early in the morning, I said to him, "We're going to see Kathy." He stopped growling, and his ears perked up. He stared at me for a moment, then slowly wagged his tail. I had to reinforce we were going to see Kathy a couple of times on the way to the airport when he thought we were headed toward the doggy jail. That, and a couple of treats along the way, garnered his cooperation for the short flight to Oahu.

After we arrived at the hospital, Kathy and Estelle were downstairs, waiting for us in the lobby. When Kathy and Pierre saw each other, I was surprised that he couldn't wait to jump from my arms to hers. I had been getting used to the idea he was my dog now. That was, until he nipped at me to release him. Obviously, he had more feelings for her–turncoat.

Their being back together was a benefit I hadn't expected. It was excellent medicine for both of them seeing each other.

After the big reunion, I escorted Kathy and Estelle to the airport. We boarded the first flight to Vegas later that morning. I doubted Cook would try to hurt Kathy again, but I wasn't taking any chances. After the plane was airborne, I said to Kathy, "I'm sorry I wasn't there to protect you."

She nodded and put her hand on my arm. "Jack, it's not your fault. Karma took care of the guy that attacked me, right?" I nodded. "Karma and a 357 Magnum. He's no longer among the living. And Cook is soon to be dealt with– I promise you."

We sat three abreast on the plane. Kathy and Pierre were next to the window. The only time during the flight Pierre looked in my direction was when he wanted another snack. Apparently, I'd been relegated to the keeper of the snacks in his world.

Six hours later, Kathy said, "I can't believe the size of the place," as she looked out the window at the metropolis below that Las Vegas had become. I understood; I remembered a time when a million fewer people lived there, and steak and eggs could be had for 99¢.

· · ·

"Make yourselves at home. This is your new home for as long as you want. I'll be going back to work soon, and you guys can be the live-in caretakers of Pierre and the property."

Estelle's brow furrowed. "We're not looking for a free ride, Jack. We'll stay here just until I can get back on my feet while Kathy's rehabilitating. Then we'll find our own place."

I pointed at Pierre. "You don't have to find a job or a place if you don't want to. I have one for both of you if you want it."

Kathy and Estelle both looked puzzled until I explained Pierre was the golden goose, so to speak.

I continued, "I'm getting paid a ridiculously stupid amount of money to take care of him, and I'm willing to share it with you guys. Besides, he seems to like you both more than me."

Kathy, Estelle, and Pierre looked like the three musketeers when I said goodbye. They were all set with a lakefront view and a month's worth of groceries.

"I'll be back when Cook has been dealt with. I don't know how long that will be. But I promise the next time you see me, you'll never have to worry about him again." I boarded the next flight to Kona to deal with Cook.

CHAPTER TWENTY-FIVE

The flight back to Kona left me unsettled. Even though Kathy said she was okay, I sensed a deep fear in her. I knew it directly resulted from Aldrich Cook not being held to account for his crimes.

I worried she wouldn't rest until he was locked up or dead. Whichever came first was fine by me. Miles didn't deserve to be murdered and Kathy to be attacked. She also didn't deserve to live the rest of her life terrified that Cook would come back to finish the job. It pissed me off just thinking about it.

The thought I couldn't let go of was the justice system had failed unforgivably one more time. This time, it was people I cared about, not strangers that I'd read about in the paper.

The stolen video; strike one. Kathy's attack; strike two. The assassination of the star witness against Cook; strike three. Cook must die was the conclusion that came to mind. He was a serial killer, free to roam the island without conse-quence. That was unacceptable to me.

The denial of justice left me no choice. Somewhere over

the middle of the Pacific Ocean, between the mainland and Hawaii, I plotted Cook's demise during the rest of the flight. By the time I saw the mountains of Hawaii off in the distance from my window seat, I'd devised a plan to erase Cook from the planet.

I promised myself he would never hurt Kathy again. As much as I wanted to go full vigilante on his ass as soon as possible, there was one more thing I wanted to try first as a last resort.

After the plane landed, I went straight to the local newspaper office. I placed a handful of classified ads to be sprinkled throughout the paper that offered a reward for the return of the stolen video of Cook attacking me at Honl's.

I paid to run the ad for two weeks. If it didn't generate any leads that led to the recovery of the video, that would be it. Cook's destiny would be a one-way trip to the bottom of the sea.

On my way home to the *Holo-Holo,* I stopped off at the post office to get my mail. There was another letter from Cook's lawyer. It was official, he was suing me. When I saw the letter, I thought maybe I should've canceled the ads and took Cook to feed the fish sooner rather than later.

When I got to the *Holo-Holo,* it felt different. Something had changed. It was too quiet. There was no Kathy, no Pierre, it was just me. It didn't feel like home anymore. For years, I'd lived alone and savored the peace that came with it. Now I missed the sound of Kathy futzing about and Pierre's toenails tapping on the deck as he followed her around the boat.

I grabbed a beer, a cigar, and a recent copy of Fishing News magazine. I headed to the fighting chair to take a break. When all else failed, that always made me feel good. With the magazine on my lap, I scanned the headlines as I lit the cigar. There wasn't anything new in the local fishing scene, from what I could see. It seemed the big marlin had all gone on vacation, and I wasn't missing much. So, that was good.

Later that afternoon, Grady had stopped by after he was off the clock. I was about half in the bag by then.

I handed him a beer as he came aboard. After he took a sip and swallowed, he said, "You remember Scott Brown–the guy with the webcam overlooking Honl's?" I nodded as I straightened up in the chair and leaned toward Grady.

"I looked into him when I found out he works in Cook's office as the IT guy, and is on parole. I called his PO, and he got me access to Brown's webcam server at the condo. Our tech guy said the server had been wiped clean. Even though it's suspicious, I don't think Brown was working with Cook when it came to the murders."

I interjected, "But Cook probably paid him to erase any video evidence." Grady nodded and said, "I think that's what happened. I just can't prove it. But I dug into Brown's background, and it turns out he served time in California and guess who his cellmate was? Cook."

"You're shitting me?"

"Nope, it turns out Cook did time for a kidnapping and rape when he was a teenager, and the state of California released him when he turned twenty-one."

"How did we not know that? Did he have an alias?"

Grady nodded. "It was back before the nationwide criminal databases. Cook was raised by his mother and went under his former stepfather's surname. She'd put him in school under that name, and when he was sixteen, he'd gotten a driver's license under that name somehow without a birth certificate.

When he committed the kidnapping and rape, he was convicted under his stepdad's surname. After he got out of jail, he ditched the stepdad's surname and started using his legal name, Cook. It was easy. All he had to do was take his birth certificate down to the DMV and get a new driver's license. Presto, he had a whole new identity. When the state of Hawaii checked his background for a real estate license, his prior history never came up."

"What was Brown in jail for?"

"He appears to be your typical white-collar criminal. Embezzlement, fraud, and a half dozen other similar crimes. He doesn't have a record for anything violent. That's why I doubt he's involved, apart from wiping the hard drive of the webcam."

Grady and I chatted over a few more beers, then called it a night. But before we did, he told me everyone was stonewalling him at work.

His investigation into the missing video was stalled. It was clear that unless someone came forward with information, the investigation was dead.

I told him about the ads I'd put in the paper. We both agreed it was a Hail Mary, but it was all we had left. Only time would tell.

CHAPTER TWENTY-SIX

Eight Days Later

It had been a week since I'd last checked in with Kathy and Estelle. I called Estelle while I had my morning coffee to get an update on how things were going in Vegas. "How's Kathy doing after her first week of rehab?" I asked.

"The good news is rehab is going well. She's writing again every day after therapy. She and Pierre sit out on the back patio and stare at the lake while she works on her book. Kathy teases they're in love and intends to get married at the Elvis drive-thru wedding chapel downtown on the strip. There's nothing wrong with her sense of humor, that's for sure."

Estelle paused, her voice cracked when she tried to continue. "The bad news is her memories from the attack have returned, and she's having nightmares. She's woken me up screaming in the middle of the night three times this week, Jack."

I wiped my eyes as I got off the phone. The guilt had returned for my failure to protect her. I wanted to grab my Glock and go to Aldrich Cook's office and erase him from the planet. He deserved nothing less than two rounds in the head and one in the chest. As much as I wanted to, I couldn't go about it that way, since I had no desire to go to prison. I had a better plan when the time was right.

My gut had been knotted up for days as the self-imposed deadline regarding Cook's fate inched closer by the minute. Beer and crackers had become my diet. Crackers to neutralize the stomach acid and beer to numb the guilt over my failure to protect Kathy.

Grady's investigation of my stolen video was officially dead. The reward I'd placed in the newspaper eight days prior had only generated one phone call. It was from a psychic. She said, for a nominal fee, she could point me in the right direction toward the stolen video. Obviously, she wasn't a real psychic. If she were, she would've known I'd hang up on her like I did.

To keep Kathy safe, I'd all but resolved myself to the fact that I had to do the last thing I wanted to. Cook was like a dog that killed chickens. He wouldn't stop. He had to be put down or locked up. Since the justice system in Hawaii was incapable of the former, the latter was the only choice left in my mind.

I swore to myself when I left Somalia, I wouldn't be a party to any more killing after I'd gotten out of the military. The last thing I wanted to do was break that vow. To protect Kathy, it was clear I had no choice.

As far as I was concerned, Cook wasn't any different from a rabid animal and had to be put down. I made up my mind, if there was a God, Cook's demise would just be one more thing I'd have to account for come Judgement Day. I could live with that.

I made a pot of coffee while I thought about it and tightened up the plan I'd thought of on the plane days earlier. I'd come up with a couple of plans I liked. My favorite was making Cook walk the plank, and then I'd chum the water and wait for the sharks to finish him. The other was more businesslike. As much as I enjoyed the thought of the sharks eating him alive, I decided on a more humane method.

I was startled when my phone rang. I'd been deep in thought about which way the ocean current would carry Cook's body after I'd shot him and dumped him in nine thousand feet of water. No need to weight him down, I thought, since the sharks would dispose of him.

I didn't recognize the number. Usually, I didn't answer unknown callers and let them go to voice mail. But since I'd placed the ads in the paper that offered a reward, I answered the phone every time it rang and paid the price for it. Hopefully, it wasn't another schmuck trying to tell me my car's warranty had expired. Those knuckleheads had no idea I didn't even own a car, and my Bronco was about fifty years past the warranty expiration date.

Instead, I was pleasantly surprised when a woman's voice said, "I'm calling about the ad in the paper concerning a stolen video. There's a reward, right?"

"Yes, if you have information that leads to the arrest and conviction of the person who stole it." There was a long pause. "What if I have the video? Would that work instead?"

When she said that, it caught me off-guard. I thought for a moment about how to proceed. I wanted somebody's ass, but I'd settle for just getting the video back, since five minutes before that I had planned Cook's death and had become willing to risk life in prison.

"That's even better. May I ask how you came to be in possession of the video, if you don't mind my asking?"

"I suspected my husband had cheated on me again, and

while I was looking for proof where I knew he hid things, I found a thumb drive with a video of someone attacking someone at the beach. I thought little about it apart from how awful it was until I saw your ad in the paper this morning. I don't know if this is the video you're looking for, but it looks like it might be."

"You bring that thumb drive to me and if it's the video I'm looking for, I'll gladly pay you the reward."

An hour later, we agreed to meet at Starbucks near the harbor. When I arrived, the place was so cold inside I would've sworn they could've hung meat from the ceiling in there. I told her I'd be seated in the corner near the entrance. What I didn't tell her was I had backup in case it was a setup to rob me.

CHAPTER TWENTY-SEVEN

I sipped a black iced tea while I waited for the woman to arrive. She wanted the reward, and I wanted the video. I wasn't the praying type, but I said one, hoping she had the stolen evidence against Cook.

I smiled when she walked through the door alone and came straight to my table. It didn't feel like I'd been set up for a rip-off, but it was better to be prepared than be a victim.

I'd worn an aloha shirt with a bright orange floral design. I'd told her to look for the ugliest Hilo Hattie's shirt she'd ever seen, and I'd be sitting in the corner.

I motioned for her to take a seat across from me, and she obliged. Her hand shook as she handed me the thumb drive. I looked at it before I plugged it into the small laptop computer that I'd brought with me. As soon as I saw it, I smiled because I knew it was mine. I'd marked it with my initials before I'd given it to the cops at Honl's beach the night Aldrich Cook had attacked me.

I looked over at Grady, stationed across the room, and

nodded. The young woman tried to bolt as he approached, but Grady blocked her escape at the door.

He cuffed her and took her to the station for questioning. Grady allowed me to watch via closed-circuit TV as he interrogated her. Her name was Gracie Jones and her husband, Mike Jones, worked in the evidence locker as a civilian employee. Jones had been at the top of Grady's list of who he suspected might have stolen the thumb drive, but couldn't prove it.

Jones had copied the drive and kept the original. He sold the copy to Cook, it turned out. After four hours of questioning, Grady didn't think Gracie was involved, and I had to agree. She didn't act guilty, and her story was consistent. Every time she repeated it, she got louder. That was consistent behavior of someone who was innocent.

After she was released without charges, I sat in the lobby and waited for her. When she came out of the interrogation room and saw me, she said, "You bastard!"

I'd expected that and didn't react. I said, "A deal's a deal," as I handed her the reward check for ten thousand dollars. She glanced at it. Her brow still furrowed as she snatched it out of my hand and headed for the door.

I trusted Grady, but I wasn't convinced Jones was the only rat that might have been involved, since Grady had narrowed it down between Jones and his co-worker. They both worked in the evidence room.

This time, before I handed the thumb drive over, I made two copies. I put one in my safe deposit box at the bank, one in my pocket, and the third one I gave to Grady to share with the Hawaii County District Attorney.

That night, Grady stopped by the boat to have a beer.

He said, "After I arrested Mike Jones, he admitted Cook paid him twenty grand to steal the thumb drive."

I interrupted, "How did Cook know Jones worked in the evidence locker?"

"Cook had sold the Jones a house the year before, and that's how he knew where Jones worked and that they were just scraping by financially. Jones had a girlfriend on the side that he'd knocked up and was desperate for money. So, when Cook floated the idea of stealing the thumb drive, Jones didn't hesitate to do it for the twenty grand."

Grady continued, "I asked him, why did you keep a copy of the thumb drive? He said he intended to blackmail Cook for more money later on."

In a toast, we clinked our beer bottles together, and I said, "One down, one rat bastard to go."

After the District Attorney watched the video of Cook attacking me, he filed an indictment for attempted murder. A warrant was issued for Cook's arrest, and Grady went looking for him. I was relieved that I didn't have to resort to becoming a vigilante.

After weeks of little sleep and frayed nerves, I felt like I could finally take a well-deserved nap. I laid down on the couch, closed my eyes, and quickly drifted off to sleep. I dreamt that Cook somehow got wind of the indictment and fled to a waiting jet at the Kona airport. The day before, he'd finally closed the sale of his office building. With millions of dollars, he no doubt was on his way to a non-extradition country. If he got off the island, the chances of catching him would be slim to none.

I partially awoke in a cold sweat, still in a dreamlike

state. I wondered for a moment if it'd really happened. That truly was a nightmare scenario that felt so real.

Thankfully, it was only a bad dream and Grady had arrested Aldrich Cook at his office building while I was asleep.

Six weeks later.

This time, the media circus outside the courthouse sensed blood in the water and had all but convicted Cook in the press. I had done my best to chum the water for the media sharks. I'd released a copy of the video of Cook attacking me to every news outlet I could find. Every night, the video played during the evening newscast.

Cook's lawyer, Tyler Blake, was on the news every night saying his client couldn't get a fair trial in Hawaii and wanted a change of venue. I didn't care if they had the trial on Mars; the video was compelling, and Cook was going to prison. It was just a matter of how long. I had no doubt this time would be different, and Cook wasn't getting out of it.

After picking the jury over a two-day period, the trial only lasted a day. The jury deliberated less than two hours. It was comprised of nine men and three women. This time, I wasn't worried that Tyler Blake would charm the women into an acquittal. The jurors were all middle-aged or older and appeared unimpressed by Blake's attempts to mesmerize them. They continuously scowled at Cook after they'd watched the video of him as he tried to stab me to death.

When the jury returned to the courtroom, Judge Clark asked the jury foreman if they had a verdict. He nodded. Clark asked, "What say you?"

"Guilty," the foreman replied. I sighed with relief that

Cook would finally be held responsible to some degree because justice had been long overdue.

A month later, Judge Clark sentenced Cook to life in prison with the possibility of parole. Cook would be sent to a prison in Eloy, Arizona to serve his time. It was where Hawaii sent all of its convicted criminals because of overcrowding at Halawa State prison on Oahu.

The thing that bothered me about the sentence was someday he'd be eligible for parole. The thought of him, a serial killer, possibly being released, had left a sour feeling in my gut. Maybe we'd get lucky and a witness in Miles' or one of the other cases would come forward someday, but I wasn't going to hold my breath.

What I was going to do was take care of some business that was long overdue.

CHAPTER TWENTY-EIGHT

The week after Cook was convicted of attempted murder, his lawyer dropped the suit against me, seeking damages for the bullet I'd put in Cook's shoulder. With that out of the way, it was time to move on and get back to being semi-retired.

For quite some time I'd thought long and hard about selling the *Holo -Holo* and moving to Lake Las Vegas. I wasn't conflicted about leaving, just whether to sell the boat.

I'd considered keeping it and leaving it in a slip at the harbor in Kona. But that would've required hiring a captain to charter it to try to cover the overhead. I'd known smart guys who'd done that and lost a ton of money. I wasn't rich, so I couldn't afford to take the risk.

Ultimately, I decided selling the boat was the right thing to do, since I had no desire to return to the island anytime soon after I left. I'd miss the old Kona, but never what it had become.

No guts, no glory, I said to myself as I called Steve

Kaiser, the local yacht broker. He had an office at the other end of the harbor.

Word around the harbor was that Steve was a wheeler dealer who had clients all over the world and could sell my boat in a short amount of time. We agreed on a sales price that I was happy with and signed a listing contract. He claimed he'd been eyeballing my boat for a while since it was a Cabo 42 and one of his favorite boats. I didn't know if it was true or not. Maybe he said that to everyone who asked him to sell their boat.

A couple of days later, I was lying on the couch in the salon of the *Holo-Holo* talking to Estelle when my phone buzzed. It was an incoming call. I saw it was Steve and told Estelle I had to go.

"Hey Jack, I got an offer for your boat. Are you ready to move?"

"Yes, who's the buyer?"

"He's a businessman from New Zealand. He's been looking for a Cabo 42 for a quite some time in Hawaii. When he saw yours listed on my website, he called right away and made a full price offer.

I emailed you the offer yesterday, but since I hadn't heard from you, I thought I'd better call you."

"Damn email, it seems the more important it is, the more likely it's gone to the spam folder."

"No worries Jack, I'll stop by with the offer in fifteen minutes if that's okay?"

"Sure, I'll be here."

Just like he said, fifteen minutes later Steve showed up with the offer. I signed it, and five days later the money was wired to my bank account.

The day before I handed over the keys, Grady and I took the *Holo -Holo* out fishing one last time. It had been months since we'd fished for marlin. We'd set up the lures just outside the harbor as we trolled south toward the fishing grounds.

Twenty minutes later, the rubber band on the starboard fishing line snapped, followed by the loud whine of the fishing reel gears. Whatever had swallowed the lure raced off in the opposite direction, simultaneously peeling off yards of fishing line as the reel spun freely. Grady was inside the cabin getting a beer when I yelled, "Fish on!"

I was up on the flybridge and shifted the boat's transmission into neutral. As the boat floundered in the light seas, I slid down the flybridge ladder into the cockpit.

I rushed to clear the stinger and port side fishing lines while Grady grabbed the starboard pole. He quickly reeled the slack out of the line. Right then, I was really missing Kathy. Normally she handled clearing the lines, and I stayed up on the flybridge maneuvering the boat.

By the time I'd gotten the lines cleared, Grady had slid into the fighting chair.

I climbed back up to the flybridge, shifted the transmission into reverse, and started backing down toward the fish.

Grady continued to crank the reel, inching the fish closer to the boat. Whatever was on the other end of the line was big, pissed off, and determined to get off the hook.

The mystery was over when the blue marlin exploded from the surface of the ocean. From its length and girth, I estimated it likely weighed at least five hundred pounds. I continued backing down the boat as Grady fought the fish that proceeded to put on a show as it breached high above the surface, twisting and turning, trying to get free. It took almost three hours to get it to the boat.

We lucked out. I was afraid that if we'd fought the fish much longer, it would've died and sank. That would've been the marlin getting the last laugh. Reeling up a dead five hundred pound fish that had sunk hundreds of feet was the last thing we wanted to do.

I had a sigh of relief when the exhausted marlin finally gave up and came alongside the boat. We tagged and released it after taking a couple of photos of the massive beast.

We took a break, drank a couple of beers, then continued to fish for a few more hours. Our luck held out and Grady caught my favorite, a forty pound mahi-mahi, plus a couple of decent sized tuna for dinner.

That evening I brought the mahi-mahi, plus fresh sashimi, to the luau at the old airport beach park. My nieces Jessica and Pua had planned it at the last minute when they got word I'd sold the *Holo- Holo*. It was my going away party before I headed off to Vegas.

When my phone vibrated, I was chatting with Sam and Jessica while we all sat at the picnic table underneath the pavilion. I didn't look to see who the caller was. I figured if it was important, they'd leave a message. When they hung up and called right back, I thought maybe I should see who it was. I pulled the phone out of my pocket and saw it was Estelle.

I said to Sam and Jessica, "I have to take this." They nodded as I stepped away toward the beach.

Estelle said, "Jack, we have a problem. Kathy and I are totally freaked out. Today she got a letter from Aldrich Cook. He sent it to her old address in Kona and it was forwarded here. He said just because he was in prison didn't mean he couldn't get to her. What does that mean?"

I glanced at my watch. "It's not her fault. It's about

revenge for me putting him in prison. I'm going to try to catch the red-eye to Las Vegas tonight. Close the blinds and stay inside until I get there. If I can't get on the next flight, I might not get there until tomorrow afternoon or later."

After I got off the phone, I told Sam and Jessica what was going on and that I had to hurry to the airport.

Sam raised his hand as I headed toward the parking lot. He said, "Hold up a minute, Jack. Let me make a quick call."

Sam had a lot of connections. I thought he was calling in a favor to get me on the next flight.

He said, "Hey Mike, we need to go to Vegas tonight." Sam looked at me and asked, "Can you be ready to leave in an hour and a half?"

I nodded. My go bag was in the rental car and ready to go. Normally, I'd kept one in the Bronco. But I'd already shipped it to the mainland after I'd sold the *Holo-Holo*.

"I don't have seventy-five grand for fuel, Sam." "Don't worry about it. This is payback for the time you called in that Black Hawk that saved Jessica's life on the beach in Puako. We know you got in a lot of trouble for that. She would've died if it hadn't been for you. Jessica smiled and nodded."

An hour and a half later, I arrived at the private side of the Kona airport. Sam's chief pilot, Mike Johnson, greeted me at the door of the Gulfstream jet as I came on board. He said, "Strap in, we'll be wheels up in just a few minutes."

As the plane made a climbing right turn over the ocean, I felt the g-forces pushing me back into the seat and the return of the knot in my gut.

CHAPTER TWENTY-NINE

The sun was just coming up when the Gulfstream jet landed at the North Las Vegas Airport. I thanked the crew for getting me where I needed to go on such short notice.

From the airport to my condo was a thirty-five minute drive. I had slept little on the plane and looked forward to seeing Kathy and Estelle before I could really rest. After I knew they were safe, I'd take a nap for a couple of hours.

When I walked through the door, I wasn't expecting the smell of bacon. Estelle was in the kitchen making breakfast. "Would you like coffee, Jack?" she said as I walked through the door. I looked around and asked, "Where's Kathy?"

"Out on the back patio, writing." My brow furrowed. So much for my instructions to stay inside, I thought. I sat my go bag down next to the breakfast bar and pulled out a stool. I took a seat and Estelle set a cup of coffee on the bar in front of me.

"Don't worry, Jack, I've kept an eye on her the entire time." I nodded as I took a sip. The nice thing about the condo was when you walked in the front door, the kitchen was on the right, then the living room. You could see from the kitchen all the way to the lake through the living room sliding glass doors.

Kathy was at the patio table with her back toward the condo. I could see her and Pierre. He looked like he was asleep in a chair next to her. "You know her, Jack. She doesn't take orders very well from anybody."

I nodded and continued to sip my coffee. It was too early in the morning to be angry, so I kept my mouth shut for the moment, though I wanted to see the letter from Cook.

Estelle must have been reading my mind. She had it in the back pocket of her jeans. She pulled it out and set it on the bar in front of me next to my cup.

"Would you like eggs and bacon, Jack?" she said without missing a beat. I shook my head as I put my reading glasses on. It was much too early in the morning for food.

With coffee and reading glasses, I was able to focus and read the short but to the point letter that Cook had sent. The envelope had his name and return address for the Arizona prison. The balls on the guy–I shook my head in disgust.

Before I took a nap, I'd make some calls and see what it would take to have Cook's ability to send mail to Kathy quashed.

It was still too early to call anyone, so I grabbed my cup and went outside to see Kathy. She started with, "I'm sorry Jack, and I know I'm not supposed to be out here. But that son-of-a-bitch will not control how I live my life."

As much as I wanted to scold her for not listening to me, I couldn't. I smiled and sat down. "I'm here. You're safe. I'll take care of it."

She smiled and nodded, then looked back down at her laptop and went back to typing. Pierre opened one eye and looked at me, then closed it. I stared at the lake while I drank my coffee and thought about what to do next.

That afternoon, the warden said all of Cook's outgoing mail would be inspected, so Kathy would never again get another letter from him.

I was satisfied with the answer until a week later, when the next one showed up. This time, it didn't have his return address on it. Somehow, he'd gotten someone on the outside to write it and send it for him.

Even though he was locked up, he had vast financial resources at his disposal. No doubt he was the richest prisoner in the state of Arizona.

I wasn't worried about him finding out where Kathy lived until one day we had an unknown visitor at the front door when we weren't home.

Estelle and I had taken Kathy to therapy. My phone pinged when the front door motion detector camera started recording a man as he approached. I wasn't expecting any deliveries, but watched to see if he left a package.

After knocking and waiting a few minutes to see if anyone was home, he tried the doorknob. I tapped the button on my phone connected to the camera audio and said, "What do you want?" He turned and bolted out of sight.

I knew we had a serious problem then. I didn't recognize him, but he had a neck tattoo of a snake that made me think he could be Russian mafia. I'd seen a similar one on a Russian mobster before.

It was evident that Cook had been busy making new friends in prison. Friends who had reach outside the prison. This guy was no random burglar.

I texted the video clip to Grady and my niece Jessica to see if, by the off chance, it was anyone they recognized.

Jessica retired from the LAPD and had worked the gang unit. She was the expert on the Russian mafia in my circle of friends and family.

Before Grady moved to Kona, he'd worked for Honolulu PD and had a fair amount of experience with the Russians. Both of them texted me back and said they didn't recognize him but would make inquiries and see what they could come up with.

CHAPTER THIRTY

Jessica called a couple of hours later and said, "I didn't recognize him, but Gabbie did. The FBI has been looking for this guy for a few years. She said he was on their radar before she retired. He's a hitter for the mob out of LA. He's not after Kathy. Cook put a contract out on you, is the word on the street. That's according to an old colleague in the agency she called. Be careful Jack, these guys are serious killers."

"Figures. Thanks, and tell her thanks for the intel."

I hung up the phone and had three pairs of eyes staring at me in the small motel room. "Don't worry, we're not staying here. Sam and Jessica said we can stay at their condo on the strip until this thing is over."

The condo was on the twenty-first floor, with a view that overlooked the Las Vegas strip. The tour helicopters that flew by at night were almost at eye level.

The next morning, I got a list of items Kathy and Estelle needed, and I headed back to Lake Las Vegas to retrieve them.

Before I went to the condo, I drove around the complex

while I looked for anyone or anything suspicious. Particularly, anyone parked down the street from my place with binoculars watching the condo.

When I saw my 96 Bronco parked outside in my assigned space, I was happy to see it had finally arrived from Hawaii. But I wasn't happy the shipping company had failed to notify me it had been delivered.

I parked Estelle's Chevy Malibu next to the Bronco and stepped out of the car. When I accidentally dropped the car keys, I bent down to grab them, and noticed something out of the corner of my eye that made me freeze. Underneath the Bronco, I saw what looked like a spark plug wire hanging down near the gas tank. Every nerve in my body said run. But I knew it was too late for that.

If a hitman was watching me, and he'd rigged a bomb with a cell phone detonator, I would've already been dead. I opened the hatch to the gas cap on the Bronco and found the end of the cable had a spark plug attached to it. The cap was gone, which allowed gas fumes to escape. Lucky for me, I saw the cable hanging down. If I had started the Bronco, it would've fired the spark plug and I would've been toast. Burnt toast. I disconnected the spark plug and removed the wire.

I was almost at the front door of the condo when a bullet whizzed by my head and blew through the front door. I ducked behind a pillar of the building for cover. As I looked at the hole in the door from the bullet, I was grateful it wasn't in the back of my skull.

To counteract the adrenaline coursing through my veins, I exhaled slowly, then released all the air from my lungs. I inhaled as I counted to four and held my breath for another count of four to get control of myself.

While I did a few more reps of combat breathing, a

thought occurred to me. I was fortunate. The hitman had missed twice. I should've been dead by now. I noted I should go gambling afterward if I lived, since it appeared I was on a streak.

It was almost funny, except for the part where he was trying to kill me. I thought I'd better do something about him before he got lucky and actually killed me.

The shot had come from a vacant building across the street that was for sale. I was safe as long as I stayed behind the pillar. For their protection, I'd left my Glock with Kathy and Estelle. My backup was inside the condo. To get it, I had to get inside without getting shot. That was the plan. Though I was safe for the moment, that didn't mean he wouldn't leave his position and come for me once he realized I was unarmed. I needed to move, and I needed to move fast. I had to go through the door, and it was now or never was the thought that rushed through my mind.

When I flung it open, I expected a burst of gunfire and hoped he'd miss again as I dove through the door. There was, and he didn't. Son-of-a-bitch that hurt. Nobody enjoys getting shot. Once again, I was glad I didn't catch one in the gourd as blood ran down my arm.

Within twenty seconds, I'd retrieved my backup from the kitchen drawer I kept it in. I grabbed a towel from in front of the stove and wrapped it around my left arm to stop the bleeding.

I was thoroughly tired of this asshole shooting at me and ran upstairs to the master bedroom, where I kept the gun safe.

He saw me through the window before I could get to the safe and fired a burst of bullets in my direction. By that time, I'd dropped to the floor and crawled across the room—I was livid. That piece of shit would not kill me in my own house.

When I got to the safe, I grabbed my AR-15 and a twelve gauge with a box of slugs. I used the shotgun to blast a hole in the wall that faced the direction the bullets had come from. Two slugs made a hole through both the interior and exterior wall, big enough that I could put my AR through it.

Even though I'd only suffered a flesh wound, it took every ounce of strength I had to pivot the gun safe from the corner to use as a shield. Its top was the perfect place to rest the AR on to use as a makeshift tripod.

I fired through the hole toward the upstairs condo across the street. I put almost a full magazine of rounds through the wall. That forced the gunman to move toward the window to return fire. When he popped up, I put him down like a duck at a carnival shooting gallery.

While I waited for the cops to arrive, I thought about how to end Cook once and for all. It was the only solution.

CHAPTER THIRTY-ONE

After I gave the cops a statement and the paramedics dressed my flesh wound, I gathered the items Kathy and Estelle had requested, got in the car and headed toward the Las Vegas strip.

Traffic was heavy, and the drive back to Sam and Jessica's condo took forty-five minutes because there was a crash on the freeway. I continued to think about what I was going to do about Aldrich Cook.

I let my mind wander as the car crept along the freeway at five miles per hour for what seemed like most of the way. Then it hit me like a bolt of lightning.

I felt giddy once I realized Hawaii housed most of its prisoners in the same prison in Arizona. That meant there was a solution to my problem.

As much as I wanted to personally stab Aldrich Cook in the heart that just wasn't going to happen, since he was in prison where I couldn't get to him.

After I returned to Sam and Jessica's place, I played twenty questions with Kathy and Estelle about the bandage on my arm. Of course, I lied about what had happened. I didn't intend to scare them anymore than they already were. After I'd convinced them it was no big deal, I set about to put a plan into action. The first step was to see if I could have a single newspaper article printed. After a few minutes of searching the internet, it appeared indeed I could, and it would be easy to do.

I'd never considered myself to be much of a writer. I was surprised by how easily the words flowed once I put pen to paper. Not only that, but I started to understand what Kathy meant when she said she felt in the zone as she'd written some parts of her book.

Though I wasn't writing a book, my words for the project I had in mind were important. I sharpened them as if I were honing the edge of a fine steel sword. They needed to do the same work. Cut quickly and to the bone.

I had a mission, and that mission was seeing to it that Aldrich Cook would never be a problem to me or anyone else here on planet earth.

Since Cook was in the custody of the Saguaro Correctional Center in Eloy, Arizona, I'd have to reach out through an intermediary. One doing time in the same facility. I knew just the man for the job. He would take a personal interest in Cook, just as I had. He had the time, the place, and the skills to solve the problem that had caused me and others a great deal of misery. It was time to reach out.

Three days later.

It was just another day in prison for Larry Johnson until he opened the letter that had been anonymously sent to him. When he unfolded the tightly creased letter, a newspaper clipping fell to the concrete floor.

It landed face up and showed an old photo of Kathy

Medeiros at the top of the clipping. The headline said that she'd been raped and murdered. He set the letter beside him on the bunk and reached down to pick the clipping up to read it. The article said how Aldrich Cook was suspected of paying Ricky Silva to carry out the attack, and that the charges against Cook had been dropped when Silva was found dead on the first day of Cook's trial.

Larry hadn't finished reading the article when he threw the clipping down and grabbed the letter. It said,

> Dear Larry,
> Who this letter is from isn't relevant. But what is important is the information contained. The facts of the matter are in the newspaper clipping I included for you to see. It's up to you to do what you want with this information. But just remember, Kathy really loved you and wanted you back... She told me she felt bad about you having to go back to prison, and that was never her intent. She told me more than once she really wanted to get back together with you and had planned to once you were released. Not only that, but she said she wanted to have your baby someday. Now, because of Aldrich Cook, that will never happen.

Larry's jaw clenched, his fists slammed into the bed, launching himself to his feet. He paced circles in his cell like the caged animal he was as the rage built inside him.

He knew who Cook was. Cook had surrounded himself

with a couple of thugs he'd paid for protection. Jesse Gomes and Billy Carvalho wouldn't be a problem because everyone knew Larry was the apex predator on the cell block.

For Gomes and Carvalho, providing security for Aldrich Cook was purely transactional. He wasn't one of them, just a haole from the mainland that had lived in Hawaii for a while and had made a lot of money. He paid, and they protected him.

Gomes and Carvalho were cousins, and like most of the Hawaiian inmates, Larry was a distant cousin. Jesse Gomes was a cousin who owed him. When they were kids, Larry had saved Jesse from drowning when he'd gotten caught in a riptide. Jesse owed Larry his life, and had promised he'd do whatever Larry wanted to repay the debt someday. Someday had come, and today would be the day Larry would call for the debt to be repaid by standing aside.

That afternoon, Larry buried a shiv in Cook's jugular in the prison yard. He bled out before the guards could get him to the infirmary. Larry was placed in confinement and arrested for murder.

CHAPTER THIRTY-TWO

We stayed a couple of weeks at Sam and Jessica's. I needed time to have the Lake Las Vegas condo repaired from all the gunshot damage. I'd made up a story about how it was a good time to have the place repainted and never let on what really happened.

That was long enough for word on the street to get around that Aldrich Cook was dead. His death nullified the contract that he'd put out on me.

When we returned to Lake Las Vegas, there wasn't any sign a massive gun battle had taken place there.

The upstairs window and the front door had both been replaced, and the bullet holes in the master bedroom walls had been repaired. It looked just as it had before Kathy and Estelle left.

My new daily routine became playing video keno and poker after I'd had my morning coffee. I liked keno because I could pick the numbers and winning seemed like it was random, unlike poker, that required a skill I didn't seem to have much of.

I was sitting at a video poker machine wondering if I

should move back to Hawaii, since I was such a lousy gambler, when Grady called.

He said, "I heard Larry Johnson won't be getting out of prison any time soon, if ever." He paused for a second, then continued, "Funny thing was how he got an anonymous letter with a phony newspaper article that said Kathy Medeiros had been raped and murdered."

"No kidding? Good thing he's not in Texas. They'd smoke him like a pack of Kools."

"He'll get life, but as far as I'm concerned, whoever sent that letter performed a community service. He's one of those guys that would've wound up back in prison for life anyway."

"Two birds, one stone." I said.

Grady thanked me for hooking him up with the part-time security gig I had in Kona and promised to stop by the next time he was in Vegas.

It was fall, and the leaves on the trees were gone. The morning temperatures had dropped into the forties. Early morning cold wasn't something I was used to. Hell, any cold wasn't something I was used to.

Larry Johnson was convicted of killing Aldrich Cook and sentenced to life without parole. Kathy would never have to worry about either of them again.

She'd finished physical therapy and had fully recovered from the stroke. We were grateful she'd not suffered any permanent physical damage. It would be a long time before the psychological damage had subsided. It would never be healed completely. There'd just be a layer of scar tissue over it. It would help her not remember the trauma so vividly.

We were all sitting at the table on the patio overlooking

Lake Las Vegas, having our morning coffee. It would be one of the last days we could do that until spring.

To keep warm, Pierre laid on Kathy's lap as she typed *The End* of her story. She looked up at me and Estelle and smiled.

"It's done."

I asked her, "Did it have a happy ending?"

She smiled again and said, "Yes, it did."

The End

EPILOGUE

As Miles had requested in his will, Jack bought property for a homeless shelter. He purchased Cook's commercial building in foreclosure and turned the property into both temporary and permanent housing. Miles stipulated twenty apartments would be free and that he'd fund the cost to the county to provide social services for those staying in the apartments while they tried to put their lives back together.

Kathy's nightmares had gone away. But her memory was still sharp from the trauma she'd gone through.

Her book was released, and it turned into a bestseller. She started dating a librarian she met at a writer's conference, who was also an accomplished author. That made Jack happy.

Kathy and Estelle continued to stay at Lake Las Vegas as caretakers of the property and Pierre. He continued to growl at Jack periodically for sport. Jack and Grady became private detectives and opened offices in Hawaii and Las Vegas.

Visit my website JeTrentBooks.com for the latest release.

ACKNOWLEDGMENTS

A Big Mahalo to Judith Shaw for the final edit. It was only because of her input that this story came out as well as it did. I'm truly blessed to have her kokua. (help)

David Berens who made the beautiful cover for the book.

ABOUT THE AUTHOR

J.E. Trent

J.E. Trent lived full time in Hawaii for over twenty two years and loves sharing his knowledge of the tropical paradise in his novels.

AFTERWORD

During the twenty-two years I lived on the Big Island, I witnessed some amazing things. Those events are where a lot of the inspiration I get comes from. My goal is to intersperse those moments in my writing, creating something unique that you can only get when you read my books.

Hawaii is a magical place. My words will never do it justice. I hope that readers take away a bit of aloha after spending time with Jack Murphy.

Mahalo for your support.

J.E. Trent

Hawi
Honokaa
Waimea
Mauna Kea
Hilo
Kona
Hawaii
Pahoa
Captain
Cook
Mauna Loa
Mountain
View
Pahala
Naalehu

BOATING GLOSSARY

Saloon = Living room. The social area of a larger boat is called the *saloon*. However, it is pronounced "salon."

Cockpit = Is a name for the location of controls of a vessel; while traditionally an open well in the deck of a boat outside any deckhouse or cabin, in modern boats they may refer to an enclosed area.

Head = Is the bathroom.

Galley = Kitchen.

Stateroom = Bedroom.

Line = Rope.

Port = Standing at the rear of a boat and looking forward, "port" refers to the entire left side of the boat.

Starboard = Standing at the rear of a boat and looking forward, "starboard" refers to the entire right side of the boat.

HAWAIIAN GLOSSARY

Mana (Ma-Na)
Spirit
Aina (Eye-Na)
Land of the island.
Honu (Ho-Nu)
It is a green sea turtle.
Malama (Ma-La-ma)
To take care of.
Hapa (Ha-Pa)
Means mixed race. Hawaiian, Chinese, Japanese, Portuguese and Filipino make up the majority of the population in Hawaii and when they marry their children are called hapa. A mixture.

Huli-huli chicken is grilled on a trailer in a parking lot or on the side of the road. It's usually related to a fundraiser.

Da-Kine (dah-KINE) is a fill-in word used for anything you can't remember the name of.

Aloha (ah-LOH-hah)

Aloha is "hello" and "goodbye." You could also have the spirit of aloha = Giving, caring.

Mahalo (mah-HA-loh)

Means "thank you."

Haole (HOW-leh)

It's used to refer to white people. It can be used offensively, but isn't always meant to be insulting. Originally it meant foreigner, but I seriously doubt anyone uses it for that anymore.

Kane (KAH-neh)

Kane refers to men or boys.

Wahine (wah-HEE-neh)

Wahine refers to women or girls.

Keiki (KAY-kee)

This word means "child." You may hear locals call their children "keiki."

Hale (HAH-leh)

Hale translates to "home" or "house." It can often refer to housing in general.

Pau (POW)

When you put the soy sauce bottle down, you may hear a local ask, "Are you pau with that?" Pau essentially means "finished" or "done."

Howzit (HOW-zit)

In Hawaii, "howzit" is a common pidgin greeting that translates to "hello" or "how are you?"

Lolo (loh-loh)

When someone calls you "lolo," they're saying you're "crazy or dumb." It's sometimes used in a teasing manner.

Ono (OH-noh)

Ono means "delicious." It can often be paired with the

pidgin word "grinds," which translates to "food." So, if you eat something delicious, you might say it's ono grinds.

Ohana (oh-HAH-nah)

Means family.

Tita (tit-uh)

Refers to a woman or teenage girl who could be said to either be a tomboy or else somewhat aggressive, tough, or rough with her language or manners.

COPYRIGHT

Copyright © 2022 by J.E. Trent

All rights reserved.

No part of this book may be reproduced in any form or by any electronic or mechanical means, including information storage and retrieval systems, without written permission from the author, except for the use of brief quotations in a book review.

This book is a work of fiction created by J.E. Trent.

www.ingramcontent.com/pod-product-compliance
Lightning Source LLC
Chambersburg PA
CBHW031025190726
48286CB00003BA/1027